By James Leo Herlihy

JAMES
LEO
HERLIHY

SIMON AND SCHUSTER / NEW YORK

A
STORY
THAT
ENDS
WITH A
SCREAM
AND
EIGHT OTHERS

"The Fright of Mrs. Yeager" was first published in *Esquire* Magazine. "Laughs, Etc." was first published in *Playboy* Magazine. "The Astral Body of a U.S. Mail Truck" was first published in *Mademoiselle* Magazine. "The Day of the Seventh Fire" was first published in the *Florida Quarterly*.

FOR OLD FRIENDS

CONTENTS

CONTENTS

"My children," said an old man to his boys, scared by a figure in the dark entry, "my children, you will never see anything worse than yourselves."

—RALPH WALDO EMERSON

A

STORY

THAT ENDS

WITH A

SCREAM

1

"**I**n other words," said Mary Ellen McClure, "please, Ivy, let me finish! In other words, you're breaking your promise. Fine. Go ahead. Break it. *Please* do! But then, let's just *say* that what you're doing is breaking a promise."

The two women were seated in plastic-strip sun chairs under the aluminum awning next to Ivy Alesandro's trailer. There was a half-moon but it had not yet risen sufficiently high to dispel much of the darkness. Someone walking past would have seen only vague silhouettes under palm trees, human shadows busy with little red lights which were the tips of cigarettes.

"All you've done just now," said Ivy, in her dark, cool voice, "is to make it perfectly clear you haven't heard a word I said."

"Oh, I heard all right," Mary Ellen said. "I can read it back word-perfect: you realize full well I'll be disappointed, but you've had second thoughts and decided you'd really rather not fool around with ouija boards."

"Because?"

"I know! Because the forces at work on them are unknown and possibly dangerous. Now was I listening or not?"

"You were listening," Ivy said, "but I'm not sure you

15

understood one thing, which is that I meant what I said. I know a little more about these matters than you do, sweetie."

"Oh? I thought you said they were unknown!"

"They are. And you're being quarrelsome." Ivy got up and went inside the trailer, where she turned on a light. She was a long, black-haired string of a woman, but she moved and spoke and behaved as if she were beautiful.

Opening the screen door, Ivy allowed more of the light from inside to fall upon Mary Ellen, who was pouting.

Mary Ellen's hair was luminous, the color of honey. Her skin shone with good health and the effects of sunlight. She was twenty-eight, almost incredibly well formed, long-legged, full-bosomed, with long tapering fingers and perfect feet. Her neck and shoulders were soft and lean, and a man looking at them was apt to imagine his own face cradled in the curves they formed. But when she spoke, the impact of these charms was lessened: Mary Ellen was a whiner. Her voice was flat, seemingly incapable of variation except in a state of emotion, when it became too high.

She said, "You want me to go?"

But she was safe, she knew Ivy was desperate for company. Sandro, Ivy's husband, was always working. He was a diver. In the daytime he dove for pieces of coral and conch shells and seahorses, various undersea things he sold to gift shops along the Keys, and in the evenings he was busy in his shed, painting and varnishing and mounting. Ivy claimed she liked having so much time free for reading (mostly occult books with unpronounceable titles), but Mary Ellen knew the poor thing loathed solitude and would do almost anything for human company. Especially now, with all the winter people gone, when time was more than ever such a sticky, heavy-hanging nuisance of a thing.

Ivy said, "I thought you wanted to do your toes this evening. Well, come on in and do your toes, for heaven's sake. You can use my Elizabeth Arden."

"Oh, no thanks." Mary Ellen stood up, putting her cigarette out with her foot. "I don't ever want you to feel you have to entertain me. I'll just go along home," she said, starting out, certain of being called back.

"Mary Ellen!"

She stopped and looked at Ivy.

"Why is it so important to you," Ivy said, "to sit down and play with a silly old ouija board? The contacts you get are almost always of a very low order. And it usually leaves me with a dreadful headache."

"But it's *interesting!*" Mary Ellen burst forth in an astonishing rush of emotion that caused her to shriek. "You know what my life is in this hideous place! Getting all dolled up every night, and for what? Just to go to the Cameo theater at closing time, so I can watch Matt put the film away. And do you know why I have to go every single night without fail? Would you like to hear why?"

She waited for encouragement from Ivy, but when none came, she went on without it.

"Because my great big hairy husband, six foot two in his stocking feet, is afraid to walk home alone! . . . Oh, now I hate myself," she added, guessing that Ivy probably hated her, too.

"I've never told that to a living soul, but it's true, Ivy. Why do you think we live down here, because of the sun? Ha! Oh no, it's because he's afraid of Chicago! He's afraid some, I don't know what, some gang of little boys I suppose, will sneak up on him and hit him. Isn't that a thrilling thing to live with, a husband that's afraid of his shadow?

And so every night at bedtime, I go for a drive to keep myself from going mad."

(Mary Ellen was not admitting to the real pleasure she took in these drives. Her favorite of all was across the Seven Mile Bridge which began at the southern end of Marathon. It was narrow and straight, and it went on and on as far as the eye could see. With the ocean on the left and the Gulf on the right, it was like driving on a tightrope across an infinity of water. Often she'd put the gas pedal all the way to the floor, determined to leave it there until she could no longer bear it, her eyes darting back and forth from the highway to the speedometer. Usually at 95, but sometimes only at 100, she would experience her favorite emotion: terror—the desirable kind, self-inflicted, and with her fate seeming still to be in her own hands.)

". . . and of course there's the supermarket. D'you know, I purposely forget things, just so I'll have an excuse to go back?" she said, omitting any mention of her highly titillating flirtation with the manager. "And every week, I have the enormous charge of walking up the highway to the launderette. Period. My life. So now does it seem so terribly hard to understand why I leap at the chance to do something a little unusual?"

"Poor darling," Ivy said, not bothering to mask very carefully the emptiness of her remark; for her mind was elsewhere.

Nor indeed was the lapse noticed by Mary Ellen. Accustomed to thinking of Ivy and herself as best friends, she was seldom troubled by the inconsistency of this view with the fact that they disliked one another intensely. Like all whiners, Mary Ellen was not truly interested in tenderness or affection. She often called her yearnings by those names because of their popularity; like famous-brand foods, they had just the right sound to her ear. But the commodity it-self was often flavorless and left her unsatisfied. She would have been much surprised to learn what underlay her attachment to Ivy, but the fact was that in that tall lady's presence Mary Ellen was in a constant and pleasurable state of fear.

Now Mary Ellen stood looking at Ivy, and there was a long silence. Ivy was still in the doorway, holding open the screen door. Lighted from behind, her face was in shadow. She wore black slacks and a black blouse, accentuating her extraordinary height and slenderness. Brass loops dangled from her ears and a green crepe de Chine scarf was tied loosely, attractively, about her head. For Mary Ellen it was one of those moments at which the most familiar person in your life can suddenly appear as a stranger: Ivy might have been a Gypsy, or a witch, or an apparition.

"Poor, poor baby," said this awesome figure in the doorway. "Come, let's go make a ouija board, shall we?"

She washed the kitchen table and dried it with a dish towel. It was made of Formica, a smooth white surface on which, with an eyebrow pencil, she printed the alphabet, the words YES and NO, and the numbers.

YES   NO

ABCDEFGHIJKLM
NOPQRSTUVWXYZ
1234567890

The women sat at either side of the table, each with her packet of cigarettes close by. Also on the table were an ashtray, a white teacup, and a pad of dime-store writing paper. Ivy held a ballpoint pen. The table was lighted by a wall bracket with a green glass shade. Under the lamp, leaning against the wall, was a steel-rimmed mirror Ivy had brought from the bathroom.

"They like to see us clearly," she explained, "and it helps them somehow if there's a mirror nearby."

"Oh, Ivy!" Mary Ellen was thrilled by this detail in the arrangements. "I just love you to death, do you realize that?"

"Darling, I may have to ask you to shut up."

Mary Ellen made much of pressing her lips together, eager to exhibit the purity of her cooperation.

Ivy turned the teacup upside down. She placed two fingers of one hand on its bottom rim, and instructed Mary Ellen to do the same, explaining that the handle would serve as a pointer.

"Now when it starts moving—" she said, "—no, not so much weight there. See? Let your hand float, it's just the fingers that rest on the cup, okay? Now, as it moves, I'll take notes and we'll separate the letters into words after each sentence. Oh-oh! Here it goes!"

The cup described a large curve across the table, moving slowly at first and then gaining speed. It was like a dancer warming up on an unfamiliar stage before a performance.

"I cannot bear this excitement," Mary Ellen said.

"You're having fun, aren't you," said Ivy, removing her hand from the cup. Then, speaking to the room at large, she said, "We are here to communicate only with sympa-

thetic spirits. Let it be understood, whoever you are, we
will not tolerate mischief, or anything unpleasant. . . ."

To Mary Ellen, Ivy now looked exactly like a fairy-
tale witch. Her eyes, big and dark-circled, roved about the
room as if they saw "things" in the air, and her thin lips
seemed perfectly at ease spilling out orders to whomever it
was she was speaking to—perhaps (who knew?) a crowd
of goblins! If she was putting on a show, she certainly
was doing a bang-up job of it.

". . . we're interested strictly in matters of knowledge
and philosophy and truth," she continued. "I say this not
because I have the slightest reason to believe the spirit
present is in any way negative or troublesome, but merely
because I consider it efficacious to state our objectives quite
clearly at the outset." She touched the cup again. "Fingers,"
she said to Mary Ellen, who quickly returned her hand to
the cup; then, "Have I made myself clear?"

The cup moved slowly at first. It pointed at the S,
moved slowly to the H, gained speed as it headed toward
I, and before it could finish the word, Ivy had risen from
the table and was reaching for her cigarette.

She seemed to Mary Ellen to be absolutely furious.

"Ivy, what's wrong?"

"Sorry, handsome!" Ivy said to the mirror, looking at
it with such power Mary Ellen half expected it to shatter.

"Ivy," she said, "if you don't tell me what is happening
here, I will scream!"

"Oh, we've got a little smarty-pants type spirit here,"
said Ivy. She told Mary Ellen which letters had been
pointed at.

Mary Ellen said, "Oh! Why, that's just terrible! Give
me one of those matches, for godsake!"

When Ivy had lighted her own cigarette, she tossed the matches to Mary Ellen, who caught them in a butter-fingered way.

"You see? They're no better than little boys," Ivy said. "And some of them just love to say naughty words in front of ladies. Only it can get plenty worse, I assure you. Why don't we just play cards." She began rummaging in a kitchen drawer.

"*Play cards!*" Mary Ellen was horrified.

Ivy found a deck. "These are awfully greasy, but you could go get yours."

"Ivy, you are trying to torture me! Admit it!"

"Oh, now, don't tell me you want to sit here and let some invisible idiot spell out a lot of dirty words for us? Is that your idea of an evening?"

"Ivy, why are you so shocked by a mere word? I've heard you use the same one yourself!"

"True, but I hope by the time I'm dead and working the other side of a ouija board, my vocabulary will have improved."

"A-*ha*, you do think it's a ghost, don't you!"

"Not necessarily."

"But you just said . . ."

"Mary Ellen, stop! I don't know what it is. I'm used to thinking of them as ghosts, that's all. But it could be you, it could be me, or one of our unconsciouses. These things are simply not known."

"Well, what difference does it make? It's fun, dammit. Come on, Ivy, please!"

"You are altogether too excited about it. That's what I don't like."

"Oh, pooh! You know it's my nature to just—throw

myself into things."

"Exactly," Ivy said, nodding vigorous agreement.

Mary Ellen put her fingers on the teacup. "Oh, Ivy, I can just feel him quivering under here, he's dying to tell me something."

Ivy returned to the chair. Her hand hovered briefly over the cup as she said, "Spirit, I hereby serve notice, I refuse to cooperate with anything wicked. If you give us messages that are in any way obscene or even unpleasant, I will open this door and smash the teacup against the pavement. And that'll be the end of your voice. Do you understand? . . . Mary Ellen," she said, glancing at the blonde, "your hand."

The cup went directly to the word YES, circled it several times. Then it began to move, pointing to a number of letters in quick succession as Ivy wrote them down.

MARYELLENISADUMBBIT

"Hold it!" Ivy said. She removed her hand from the cup and drew slashes between the words.

MARY/ELLEN/IS/A/DUMB/BIT

"Here you are, dear." She showed the not quite complete sentence to Mary Ellen.

Mary Ellen said, "Oh, Ivy, you did that yourself! For a joke!"

"Is that what you think?" Ivy's witch eyes were dancing their way into her brain.

The blonde shook her head. "You didn't."

Ivy said, "I suppose you still want to go on with this?"

"Yes!"

"If we proceed, I am not responsible for anything that happens. Agreed?"

"Oh, absolutely, Ivy. I take full responsibility."

"No matter what?"

"No matter *what!*"

The next sentence read:

I/KNOW/SOMETHING/ABOUT/MARY/ELLEN/
TEE/HEE

"Do you want to hear it?" Ivy said. "It's up to you, Mary Ellen."

"Of course! I've got nothing to hide."

"Okeydoke," said Ivy. They returned their fingers to the cup, and watched as their next sentence was formed.

MARY/ELLEN/IS/LOOKING/FOR/EZRA/EVERY/
NIGHT/IN/HER/HUSBANDS/CAR/SHE/GOES/LOOK-
ING/FOR/EZRA

When Ivy showed her the page, Mary Ellen opened her mouth wide. "Why, that's an absolute lie! Ivy, I hope you don't believe this! I don't even know anybody named Ezra!"

Ivy shrugged and said nothing.

"He's trying to give you the impression," Mary Ellen said, "that I go out picking up men!"

"Why, that's slander! An open-and-shut case! Why don't you sue?"

"Who? Oh, Ivy, you're teasing! Come on!" She put her fingers on the cup. "Ask him who Ezra is."

"It's your conversation. He's not talking to me."

"Spirit," said Mary Ellen, in a small, extremely polite voice, "would you mind very much please telling me who is this Ezra you speak of?"

The cup moved at once, and quickly.

HES/QUITE/A/GUY/BABY/HES/QUITE/A/GUY

Mary Ellen looked at the page, and then at Ivy. "What do I ask him now?"

Ivy took over. "Spirit, Mary Ellen wants to know why you said she was looking for this Ezra. What does that mean, Spirit?"

The cup moved under their fingers for several minutes, as Ivy made more notes. When she had finished dividing them into words, she pushed the pad across the table to Mary Ellen.

SHES/HAVING/TROUBLE/WITH/TIME/SHE/
DOESNT/KNOW/WHAT/TIME/IS/TIME/IS/A/SPI-
RAL/YOU/GOT/TO/RIDE/IT/EASY/SHES/SLIDING/
AROUND/ON/IT/SHE/THINKS/THERES/A/TOMOR-
ROW/SHE/THINKS/THERES/A/YESTERDAY/SHE/
DOESNT/KNOW/HOW/TO/RIDE/IT/SHE/THINKS/
TIME/IS/HER/HUSBANDS/CAR

"It's like jibberish," Mary Ellen said. "But he knows about the car! Oh, Ivy, I'm terrified!"

"Would you like to stop?"

"*No!*" she shrieked, putting her fingers on the cup. "Come on!"

"I just hope," Ivy said, "that he won't get too long-winded. I'm getting a headache."

"Come *on*, Ivy."

"And you couldn't care less, could you?"

"About what?"

"Nothing." Ivy picked up her pen, taking more notes as the cup moved with what appeared to be deliberate slowness.

EZRAIS

"Get moving, spirit!" Ivy said, irritably. Mary Ellen admired her courage; but the cup did not alter its pace. When the sentence was completed, Ivy read it aloud to Mary Ellen.

" 'Ezra is waiting for you.' "

Now Mary Ellen's voice was a mixture of gentle wheedling and desperate curiosity. "Spirit, I'm begging you to tell me: Who! Is! Ezra!"

The next group of letters was spelled with such speed that Ivy commented on the difficulty of getting them down on paper. And when it had pointed to the last letter, an M, the cup rushed to the opposite side of the table and fell to the floor. Neither of the women could catch it. They looked at the broken teacup for a moment and then their eyes met. Ivy shook her head.

"Why are you doing that?" Mary Ellen asked. "Why are you shaking your head?"

"I don't like this," Ivy said, "anything about it. Not one bit."

"Ivy, please, you are scaring me to death! I am absolutely terrified. Stop looking at me that way. I'm begging you: stop!"

Ivy closed her eyes and pressed them with the tips of her fingers.

"What don't you like?" Mary Ellen asked. "Tell me!"

"I don't like this headache," Ivy said. "What did you think I meant?"

"No, no, it was something about that last thing he said. You haven't showed it to me! Why?"

Ivy looked at the paper. "What, this?" She placed slashes between the words, and pushed it across the table to Mary Ellen.

It read: YOULL/KNOW/HIM/WHEN/YOU/SEE/HIM

"That's nothing very earth-shaking, is it?" Ivy said.

She rose from the table and went to the kitchen sink,

where she drew a glass of water and swallowed three aspirin tablets.

2

"**A**ren't we happy?" said Matt McClure the following morning. "I thought we were happy."

"We are, Matt, we are very happy," Mary Ellen said.

Matt was sitting on the edge of the bed, naked, looking for his socks.

"They're under it," his wife said. The trailer was laid out in such a way that she could see easily into the bedroom from the kitchen, where she was rooting through the dishpan in search of cups to wash.

"Under what?"

"Oh, well now, let's see, they're under my *foot!* The bed, Matt, the bed! There's nothing else in there, is there? For them to be under?"

Matt found his socks and shook them out. "Let's get back onto this subject we're talking about, Mouse. Let's get back onto this happiness subject. It sure does come as a surprise to hear about how bored and miserable my wife is."

"Oh, honestly! That's what I *said* to her! To get her to do this ouija board thing with me. Good lord, Matt!"

"Well, that's just charming, having people run all over this island thinking we're not happy people. I wonder if I have any clean ones, do you suppose there's any clean?"

"You *know* there aren't!"

Alarmed at her tone, Matt came into the kitchen saying, "Hey, I'm not mad at the Mouse, is the Mouse mad at me?"

"Yes, she is. She tells you about a very terrifying experience and all you can do is make her feel awful and guilty and just rotten about there not being any socks fresh. Yes, she's mad! As a hornet!"

"Aww." Matt put his arms around her, the socks dangling in the sink. "Listen here, what do you think this is? I love my happy Mouse."

"Matt." Mary Ellen's voice was low, carefully contained. "Matt, the entire world has a perfect view of your rear end through that screen door. Will you put some pants on, please?"

"Not until we're happy."

"We are happy," she said through her teeth.

Matt, satisfied, went into the bedroom and came out a moment later, barefooted, zipping up his trousers. "So anyway," he said, "you did this ouija board thing with her, and what?"

Mary Ellen was seated at the little table next to the window, having her coffee and a cigarette. As Matt filled his own cup, she said, "Oh, nothing, except that your dear friend, Ivy Alesandro, who you think is so marvelous, tried to scare me, and succeeded, half to death. I mean *me* half to death."

"Ivy?" Matt sat across from Mary Ellen, and took one of her cigarettes.

"No, her grandmother! . . . On second thought, I will say, sitting there talking to a ghost, she looked like somebody's grandmother. Or a witch. Do you realize Ivy looks very much like a witch? Think about that hair for a minute."

"Did she say it was a ghost?"

"And that *chin!* . . . Oh, she didn't say. But if she was talking to it, and there was nothing there, what was I supposed to think?"

"I don't know, but it sounds morbid," Matt said.

"Do you realize she has no mouth either? Ivy has no mouth whatever. I don't know how she takes *nourishment!*" Mary Ellen took a fresh cigarette and lit it from the one she'd been smoking. "Oh, but *excuse* me! You think she's just stunning; I forgot!"

"Oh, now, I don't know. I always liked her, but I never went ape. Haven't I always admitted that? We've known she takes sleeping pills, we've discussed her imagination before, we've discussed her plenty." Matt shook his head, narrowed his eyes reflectively. "No, I don't care for this thing. This whole thing's got a morbid tang to it."

"What're you talking about, Matt?"

"I'm just saying, if you decide to see a little less of her, it's okay by me, I'm not ape on the subject of Ivy."

"See less of her!" Mary Ellen nearly choked on her cigarette smoke. "You have to be kidding, Matt."

"I just mean, whatever you want, because if she's going to go around getting morbid on you, you don't have to take it."

"Matt, we are talking about my best friend in the world!"

"Now, look, I only mean, whatever you want is all."

"Let me tell you, then. I think it would be nice to be able to discuss Ivy's flaws without my husband forbidding me to see her."

"Fine by me. Listen, kid, I'm with you. All right?"

She nodded.

"Can I see a little crockery now?" Matt said. "A little bridgework?"

"Matt, please do not make me smile. I am a very happy woman but I do not like to smile every second. Besides, we are trying to discuss something."

"Mmm, but I hear better and think straighter if I see a little white first. Could you, without actually smiling or anything, could you just hoist the lip and give me a little shot of white?"

Mary Ellen, amused in spite of herself, said, "Oh, Matt," giving him a smile simultaneously and with no conscious effort at all.

She then told him a version of what had taken place the night before: Ivy had deliberately pushed the teacup around, forcing the ouija board to say that a sex fiend named Ezra was lying in wait for her somewhere on the Florida Keys.

Matt was incensed. He raved and banged the table with the flat of his hand, spilled his coffee, apologized, raved some more as he cleaned it up, and declared, "This is no longer your little old garden-variety prank, this is a terrible business! Where is this Alesandro woman?" He shouted toward the door. "I'm going over there and beard this woman in her trailer, I'm going over there in person and squelch this thing, right now, in the bud!" He looked at his feet, adding, "Barefooted, if necessary!"

His rage was so impressive, in fact, that Mary Ellen was forced to quiet him with another lie: that it really was just a good joke, a fairly spooky one of course, but she and Ivy had laughed about it at the end of the evening and it'd be much better never to bring the matter up again.

Confused by the contradictions in his wife's stories, and eager of course to avoid any such ugly confrontation with Ivy, Matt was easy to persuade. He spent the morn-

ing washing dishes and getting ready for his weekly trip
to the launderette.

All through the ritual misery of her midday sunbath,
Mary Ellen labored to arrive at one of two simple views of
what had taken place the night before: either she was to
have a mysterious and thrilling rendezvous with someone
called Ezra, terribly soon, or she had been defrauded by
Ivy. Having a mind that dealt only in terms of either-or
possibilities, no other occurred to her.

At first she convinced herself that Ivy had staged the
entire episode. But then why had she appeared to be so
bitterly reluctant throughout? Simple! Because she knew
good and well, the witch, that Mary Ellen would never
have ceased imploring her to give a demonstration on the
ouija board. Ivy was a brilliant woman, it was known all
through the trailer park that she had this fabulous mind.
And obviously she was experienced in casting spells of some
sort. Ugly women had to be. And, sad though it might be,
friend or no, Ivy was plainly in that category. People always commented on how queer it was that a woman like
her could catch such a marvelously handsome husband as
Sandro. And not only catch him but hold him.

Not that there was any such thing as witchcraft.

But what else would you call it?

On the other hand, Mary Ellen really had felt some
third presence under that teacup, and there was something
about the way Ivy looked when she spoke to it, whatever
it was, something in her manner that—well, nobody could
act that well! Furthermore, Mary Ellen had been so genuinely moved by the experience that later, as she was having
her pre-bedtime drive, she felt she had recognized some-

thing actually fateful in the entire aspect of the Seven Mile Bridge, a quality she'd always been aware of but had somehow failed to give any real thought to.

It had occurred to her more than once that if ever the car were to break down in the middle of it, she'd be at the absolute mercy of anyone who stopped to help. There were always night fishermen, at least one, on the catwalks on the sides of the bridge. How many times had she been surprised almost to terror as her headlights suddenly illuminated one of these dark figures? How could she be certain one of them wasn't named Ezra, that he hadn't somehow learned of her night drives and wasn't awaiting the moment at which her luck would fail?

The thought thrilled her. She gave herself briefly to the fantasy of this lone man, pretending to be a fisherman —she made him a Cuban with a Castro beard and white-white teeth—who approaches her stalled convertible, slowly, easily, reveling in his advantage. She locks the car doors and pulls the switch under the dashboard that makes the top go up. But the rapist is an expert in nightmare timing: as the top is almost closed over her, within seconds of being too late, he arrives! With one hand and little effort, he rips back the top. Mary Ellen screams, but there's no one there to hear. And since she's been told that beyond a certain sensible point, it's fatal to resist . . .

The fantasy was exhausting.

When it ended, Mary Ellen was in a foul mood. The world had never appeared to her more flat, more ugly, more real. Everything she saw, even the sky and the hibiscus, was as commonplace as one great empty beer can, and in light of this reality, she felt thoroughly humiliated at her own gullibility the night before. She'd been a perfect foil for Ivy's spook show.

All the force of the amazement she'd felt then was transformed now into a desire to get back at Ivy, to re-establish herself on an equal footing with her. How could they be friends any more if one of them, herself, was such a fool she couldn't even hold her head up?

Suddenly disgusted with the sun, too, she took her terry-cloth robe and headed for the communal bathhouse.

Under the shower, a strategy occurred to her, a perfect one and utterly simple: she would do nothing at all. She'd visit Ivy later in the day—she often dropped by for no reason at all—and make no reference whatever to the preceding evening. If Ivy brought it up, she might even pretend she'd forgotten it entirely. Mary Ellen was delighted. She was certain the effects of this behavior upon Ivy would be devastating.

She turned off the hot water, letting the cold gradually take over her body as she chuckled and shivered and embraced herself. By the time she was dry, she knew exactly what she'd be wearing, and just what fantastic thing she'd have done with her hair when she presented herself, a vision of coolness, at Ivy's trailer later in the afternoon.

"Ivy!" she called through the screen door, which was locked. "Ivy!"

There was no answer. She went to the rear of the trailer, calling softly into the bedroom window: "Ivy? Ivy, dear, do you know it's after four?"

"Mary Ellen?" Ivy's voice was cool and low.

"Ivy, your screen door is locked."

"I'm lying down. Mary Ellen, tell me, were we supposed to do something, or what? I can't remember a thing with this headache."

Headache, ha, thought Mary Ellen. Ivy had told her

dozens of times that severe headaches often followed mediumistic activities, and presumably the ratio was: the more severe the headache, the more legitimate the "contact" had been. Mary Ellen knew a four-letter word that covered such mumbo-jumbo, and she thought of saying it now.

"No," she said instead, "we didn't have a date or anything." She looked down at her bright pink toreadors and Italian sandals to match. "I just wanted to show you my hair and all, but it doesn't matter."

"You've got perfectly lovely hair," said Ivy.

Mary Ellen couldn't see inside and wondered if she were being watched. The uncertainty made her uneasy. "I'm sorry you're having a headache," she said, immediately regretting having acknowledged it at all.

"What?" Ivy said.

She spoke a little louder this time and tried to sound skeptical. "So you're having a headache, huh?"

"A wowser."

"Anything I can do?" Mary Ellen hoped her solicitude seemed false.

But Ivy asked, "Like what?"

"Well, I could get you an aspirin."

"Oh, baby, I've got myself *lined* with aspirin. But if you've got some nice heroin out there, we can maybe talk turkey."

"Some what?"

"Nothing," Ivy said. "I just said, do you mind if I don't get up and open the door. I've got this ice pack on."

"That's not what you said."

"Said when?"

"It certainly didn't sound like that to me."

"I guess it's the acoustics," Ivy said.

"This is a very peculiar conversation!"

"Me, too."

"Me, too, *what?*" Mary Ellen demanded.

"I feel peculiar, too."

"I didn't say I felt peculiar," the blonde disclaimed loudly. "I've never felt better or cooler or less peculiar in my life!" She cautioned herself against overplaying.

"Well, that's amazing. Everybody else is dying of the heat."

"The *heat!*"

"You are original, sweetheart," Ivy said. "Don't you know it's ninety-two in the shade?"

So they were talking about the weather! Mary Ellen felt the ground being pulled out from under her. Would she ever, in a bout with Ivy, actually win? It seemed unlikely.

"Ivy. I'm leaving."

"Wait, Mary Ellen." (Ivy could always be counted on to find something more to say if you'd just threaten to walk away from her.)

"Yes?"

"Darling, you haven't worried any more about last night, have you?"

It looked as if Mary Ellen were actually being given an opportunity to play her scene; she told herself to proceed cautiously.

"Last night?" she said, with just the right amount of puzzlement in her inflection.

"All that nonsense about Ezra on the ouija board," Ivy said.

"Oh, *that!*"

"It was fun though, wasn't it?"

"Oh, oodles! But I'd forgotten all about it."

"That's nice," Ivy said. "Bye, darling."

"Bye!" Mary Ellen's voice was candy, but if her eyes had been weapons of destruction, the Alesandro trailer would have melted on the spot and Ivy would have been left dying a slow death covered with hideous, lavender-colored sores.

Mary Ellen walked away exhausted, soaked in her own perspiration; the dissolved glue in her hair trickled down her forehead and the back of her neck.

Ivy's cool dismissal of last night's "nonsense" had done nothing more than revive her own deep certainty that the teacup oracle had spoken the truth.

Her emotions were a mess: she was delighted that this mysterious, thrilling trouble still lurked ahead for her, annoyed that it was out of her control, furious with Ivy on unspecific grounds, frustrated in her marriage, and miserable about the collapse of her hairdo. For a moment, it seemed as if she might cry, but in her state, coveting violence, tears would have been a galling compromise.

A motorcycle passed by on the highway, and she thought how glorious it would be to be riding on it stark-naked, to go blazing down the Keys squashing everything in her path, leaving behind her a wake of horror and bloodshed and shock. The idea thrilled her. She stopped and looked and saw herself clear as day, approaching from the north. The roar of her jet-black motor was tremendous and there she was astride it, hair trailing behind her like a torn blond flag, pretty pink-tipped boobies to the wind, splendid suntanned thighs gripping the saddle. Men and women stood in awe along the highway, hawks and sea-birds and even flies stopped dead mid-flight to look down, and chickens and dogs and children scattered to make a path for this glory of blond flesh streaking through their lives on its terrible black machine. Taking a closer look at her fantasy, Mary Ellen saw that she was not alone on the motorcycle. She was on the buddy seat clinging to the figure of a man clad in black leather from helmet to boots. His goggles covered most of his face and the rest of it was indistinguishable. But of course she knew at once who he was.

Ezra moved into her mind in such a bold and familiar way as to make it perfectly clear he had no intention of leaving. It was as if her life had been taken over by the Mr. Blank of dreams—that super-familiar person of the night whose exact identity is never quite revealed, but who usually vanishes before the morning coffee.

But Ezra did not leave, and Mary Ellen moved through the rest of the afternoon in this agonizing, tantalized state, seeing him, not seeing him.

In her own trailer again, she sat perfectly still, trying to hear his voice, hoping his speech would trigger the entire image into focus. She tried to make him say, "You remember me, baby, I'm Ezra, the guy that . . ." and trick him into telling her how they would know one another, where they would meet and what ghastly, splendid thing would transpire between them.

Matt cooked a superb spaghetti sauce for their dinner, but his wife ate it as if it had come from a can. He was offended and said so. Mary Ellen then assured him it was a terrific sauce, it really was. But her eyes were big and glassy and unfocused.

When the time came for Matt to open the movie house, she said she thought she'd like to go with him, even though she'd seen the entire double feature two nights ago and hadn't liked it at all.

For a while she sat upstairs in the projection room with Matt. The first film was some damn foreign thing, very artsy-pooh, with practically no women in it. At odd moments her mind was caught up with the little beam of light issuing from the projector. She said something to Matt about how amazing it was that when the light hit the screen it was all sorted out into objects and people. And oh, of course, he took the opportunity to launch at once into a dissertation, endless it seemed to her but no doubt very manly, about the physics of light, thanks oodles, so she went downstairs and sat for a while in the back row, studying the backs of heads.

The theater was full of possible Ezras. At one point she wandered down to the front row and walked slowly back up the aisle to scan the faces, but they were all either familiar or ordinary or both. Forcing herself to sit down, she saw one heaven preview, with Sophia Loren walking in a torn dress but like a queen through the rubble of some war, looking as if she were about to spit in God's eye. Great! But that was tomorrow's film. Then the second full-length boredom commenced, this one made in England and in English at least, but the voices were all very raw-thur and the clothes were just really and truly awful and got even worse to the extent that her nerves were soon near the breaking point. So she went back upstairs and told Matt that even though she was a fantastically happy woman, she thought she'd like to cry for a while, just for fun, if he'd please kindly shut up and hold her. And Matt held her. But it was no help at all, for she was unable to cry. Somehow, the next hour did pass; how, she couldn't honestly have said. But the film did end at last and Matt closed the theater.

They went home, and Matt went straight for the television and turned it on.

Mary Ellen stood in front of the set and said, "I do not wish to believe this."

"What?"

"That you're going to watch TV. I see it. But I do not believe it. My eyes are goddam liars."

"Now look, just listen," Matt said. "I had no intention of looking at TV. All I did was turn it on. Did you think I was going to look at it, for godsake?"

Mary Ellen went to the refrigerator, opened a can of beer and took a good long swig from it.

"Right out of the can?" Matt asked.

"That's right," she said, "right out of the can. Give me the car keys."

"Why, where, what're you going to do?"

"Don't I always take a drive?"

"In this *mood?*"

She held out her hand. "Keys keys keys."

"They're in the car."

She went out to the driveway. Matt followed her, saying, "Honey, I'm scared."

Mary Ellen got into the car, and as she backed out into the lane, Matt ran alongside, holding onto the door handle, pleading with his face and his voice, "Mouse, Mouse, Mouse!"

She stopped to shift into drive. Matt reached in with his left hand and grabbed the wheel. "Mouse, please!" he said. "What're you going to do?"

She held the burning end of her cigarette within an

inch of his wrist and looked at him threateningly. "Let go," she said. "You can go inside if you're scared, and lock the door."

Matt removed his hand from the wheel. "Oh, that's what you think, you think I'm scared, is that it?"

The car moved forward.

"When are you coming back?" he shouted.

"When I find Ezra!"

Matt ran down the lane after the car, ran all the way to the highway, calling "Mouse, Mouse, Mouse!"

3

Mary Ellen spent the next two hours doing the highway. She started at the northbound bridge and drove south, stopping along the Gulf side at every snack bar and Dairy Queen and luncheonette and roadhouse, following an invented hunch, one in which she could pretend to only a shred of faith, that on some barstool or banquette, at some table in a corner, in some parked car, *somewhere,* she would find a face that would fill the bill. At each spot her faith lessened as her desperation increased, and soon she was on the Seven Mile Bridge, racing toward Key West. Out of habit, she pressed the accelerator all the way to the floorboard, wondering, at 95 miles an hour, if speed had lost its power to thrill her. She felt nothing. And since 100 was no better, she kept her foot down and soon the needle was dancing between 105 and 110. For a moment the numbers themselves caused some excitement, but the experience of speed seemed no keener now than at 55 or 60.

And wouldn't you know! she thought, as she heard the

siren and saw through the rearview mirror the whirling red light on top of the car behind her, that on the very night when it had ceased being the least bit of fun, they'd catch her?

There was a beer can on the seat next to her. She slowed down and gave it a toss, intending for it to go over the guardrail into the water, but it went clattering instead along the pavement behind her.

She stopped and waited.

Through the mirror she saw the police car stop behind her. The door opened. A dark, uniformed man emerged from it. As he moved toward her, no longer in range of the mirror, Mary Ellen's eyes dropped to the steering wheel, which she held tight in her hands. Then a shadow fell across the wheel and an oily dark voice began to enter her, telling her to get out of the car. But she wasn't listening to the words. She saw her own hands loosen their grip on the wheel as she sat back in the seat, thinking, *If I'm merely being arrested for speeding, why do I shake like this?*

Mary Ellen then experienced something, a hunch or a hope or a vague feeling, that once she looked at the policeman, nothing would be the same again, ever. This sensation was at once frightening and entirely welcome. She was smiling as she turned her head toward the man to whom had been given this importance.

As he continued to press his voice into her, deeper and deeper, a warm black viscous thing that used phrases like beer can and speed limit and driver's license to find more and more secret openings through which to penetrate, she encouraged him with her eyes. Mary Ellen could have made no clear utterance in actual speech, but her eyes chattered away with their simple blue eloquence, telling him how much she admired tough, glittering eyes like his, and tanned, coarse skin; and they made it perfectly clear that a thick, cruel mouth is more exciting than ever when its upper lip is all but covered by a heavy, bristling black mustache. In a word, said her eyes, his manliness was the most awesome thing she'd ever encountered. And they told the truth. Therefore, with such pure, wordless communication taking place, it was not at all surprising that he would open the car door, or that she would move over to make room for him in the driver's seat.

She probably wouldn't have touched him, certainly not so boldly, if it hadn't been for the signet ring. She first became aware of it as he placed his dark, hairy hand on the steering wheel. She reached up and took the hand in both of her own in order to read the initials:

EG

The *E* of course caused everything to click into place.

Matt sat for a long while in the patio, feeling too hurt and deserted to think very much about the dangers of the dark. But as time passed, he found himself studying, perhaps by force of habit, or character, the shapes of the trees and flowers and bushes, things he himself had planted with such gentle, almost obsessive care, wondering how the absence of sunlight on them could cause them to assume such dreadful aspects. Flower beds became prone monsters and blossoms were warts on their lumpy, green hides. Banana trees were still banana trees but now their great leaves shielded the terrible redheaded dwarfs that night had made of the ixora bushes and the crotons; and breezes carried along their grisly whispered plans to other ugly night things. Matt soon found himself sitting in a bolt-upright position, hands caught in his crotch, pressed between his tense thighs, and though he knew the real name and harmless, lovely, daytime face of every awful thing in the court, all his good sense was useless to him now. For his eyes and ears were no longer hooked up to his power of reason. Something alien had hold of them. He knew this terror under the name of night, a gruesome thing to be frozen inside of, all alone. His wife was in it, too, but in some other part of it, damn her, and not frozen either. She was moving free and easy through it; she wasn't afraid of the night, hell no, she was out to join it, *out to join it!* This thought carried with it a special new wave of terror that caused Matt to challenge himself into motion, and somehow he was able then to walk out into the dark, toward company, toward the Alesandro trailer.

"Sweetheart," said the policeman, "what we're gonna do now is this." But for a moment, he said nothing more, just pulled on his cigarette and looked at the sky. He was lying on a beach towel they'd found in the back seat. Mary Ellen was standing naked in the sand, looking down, slapping absently at sand flies.

"Please say your real first name," she said. "Please. That's all I ask."

"I said it. I said it was Eddy. I said it twenty-nine times. And then I changed the subject."

"But the truth! Oh, please!"

He looked at her for a moment, but she was between him and the moon and her face was in shadow. "Why don't you get back down here a second?" he said. "We got to come up with a plan."

"Please," Mary Ellen said, "the second letter is a Z, isn't it?"

The policeman threw his cigarette in the direction of

the water, then he sat up and began to button his shirt. "What we'll do, now listen, we'll get to a phone booth, that's A. You'll drop me at a phone booth, and B is you'll drive home alone. You can do that, can't you? Under ninety-five, *por favor?* And I'll get one of the guys to pick me up. That shouldn't foul me up, should it?"

Mary Ellen said nothing.

"Or you either. I'm thinking of you. We don't want to foul you up either. You know a ticket for that speed'd cost you a good hundred? So you're lucky, all you got to do is keep still. Now me: you know what I got to come up with? I got to come up with how come I didn't take you in."

The policeman stood up and took hold of her again; both hands at her waist. "But you were special," he said. "Listen, I wouldn't even care if they suspend me. And I want you to know I appreciate . . ."

At just after two in the morning, Mary Ellen knocked lightly on the door of Ivy Alesandro's trailer.

Ivy, her face chalk-white, almost blue in the moon-light, a benign, compassionate mask, pushed open the screen almost at once and stood before her, taller than ever. Smiling. Concerned. Arms outstretched, lots of bracelets jangling, cigarette holder sparkling like a wand, and smoke of course, smoke rising from her hand and from every opening in her head.

And through it all her voice, lower, more liquid than ever: *"Mary Ellen McClure!"*

She stepped down into the patio, closed the door gently. "Where on earth have you been?" she said.

Mary Ellen simply stood there. She was barefooted,

carrying one sandal, the other apparently lost, her face smeared with old makeup. She'd made some effort to restore order to her hair without a comb, but to no avail. Her eyes were cold, deadly.

"You look like a wild woman!" Ivy said. "Are you all right?"

"Where's my husband?"

"He's in the bedroom. Sandro's giving him a rubdown, he's wonderful with hysterics. Sweetie, you really shouldn't leave him like that. He came to us in an awful state, shaking head to foot!"

Ivy glanced behind her at the trailer, lowering her voice to an even more conspiratorial level. "Mary Ellen, he told Sandro an extraordinary thing. He said—and I don't believe it for a minute, I won't allow myself to! . . . Do you know what he told Sandro? That you'd gone out to look for . . ."

"Shut up shut up shut up shut up shut up!" Mary Ellen continued to say these words over and over again until she ran out of breath.

But Ivy was unperturbed. She smiled and touched Mary Ellen's cheek. "Poor, poor baby," she said, as Mary Ellen backed away.

Still smiling, Ivy opened the door and called cheerfully, "Sandro?"

When her husband answered, she said, "Sandro, would you tell Matt to guess what darling person is here asking for him, fit as a fiddle?"

Mary Ellen decided at once to go for her throat. The decision and the action took place within the same split second, so that by the time Sandro and Matt emerged from the trailer, the two women were on the ground, Mary

Ellen on top. Ivy was ineffective in protecting herself. She didn't even scream, just made a small gagging sound as Mary Ellen's thumbs pressed into her throat.

Matt took hold of Mary Ellen's waist and began pulling while Sandro, a powerfully built blond Italian, forced her hands away from Ivy's neck. Then the four of them were talking at once. Mary Ellen saying, "I hope I killed her, did I kill her?" Sandro saying, "What the hell's wrong with that woman?" Matt saying, "Mouse, Mouse, what's happening to my little Mouse?" And Ivy, holding her own throat, eyes ablaze, saying, "Don't anybody take a step, my earring's gone."

Sandro helped Ivy to her feet and held her in one big arm, pointing at Mary Ellen with the thumb of his free hand and looking at Matt, saying, "Get that woman out of here fast." But Mary Ellen was shouting, "Her earring! Did you hear that?" and Sandro had to repeat his order, "Get her out of here, Matt."

Matt was scared. "Listen, this is all just some misunderstanding," he said, his voice shaking as he led Mary Ellen out to the lane. Looking back, he saw Sandro watching him. "Honestly, that's all this thing is," Matt said.

Sandro said, "*Keep* her out of here, too. That goes for tomorrow, and next month, and next year."

Mary Ellen was breathing heavily, and Matt noticed that her body temperature was high. She walked easily and with a long stride, apparently not at all weakened by what had taken place; in fact, she seemed exhilarated. Her eyes were still wild.

Arriving at their own trailer, Mary Ellen stopped at the driveway. Matt tried to guide her toward the door, but she was immovable. Between her teeth she said, "Don't you dare take me in there."

Matt wanted to tell her there was nothing to be afraid of in their little house of love, but some kind of wisdom kept his mouth closed and after a moment he released his grip on her shoulders.

She walked down the lane as Matt watched, wondering what to do. At the highway, she turned, moved along the edge of it, headed south. He began to follow, a few paces behind. There was some crazy perseverance in her stride that made him wonder if she'd keep walking forever.

But Mary Ellen didn't know any more than he did about what she was doing or where she was going. She was much too tired to be walking like this, but the alternatives, especially going home, resting, being still, sleeping, seemed unthinkable. Nor could she walk with her eyes closed. Yet she hated everything in sight, the A & P, the Dairy Queen, the Gulf station, the parked cars, the storage tanks. Every single man-made thing she looked at was like one more piece of candy to a sufferer from nausea, another sickly colored sweet thrown away by some pampered, giant infant.

And so she raised her eyes, not out of any desire to look at the sky, but out of a necessity for un-seeing the world. And there were all the stars to be confronted. They'd been waiting there to get at her eyes, millions of them waiting for millions of years, cool and utterly silent. Perhaps it was this silence in the sky that caused a new rush of panic. She threw back her head, thinking, *I'll open my mouth and scream and then Matt will have to do something about me,* and before the thought was completed, she had stopped walking and was drawing a very deep breath, determined to make a real noise, one that would count for something.

LOVE
AND THE
BUFFALO

Mr. Highet was disposed of yesterday. The other two men in here have already been . . . No, let's just say the rest of the ward is empty.

Anyway, now that I'm alone I can take some notes. I don't know how I'll get them outside. But the first real task is to get them on paper and keep them well hidden. Time enough later to worry about getting them into the hands of someone who can put them to good use.

The minute I opened my eyes this morning I knew this was it, my last day. I knew even before Miss Z came in and did her smile. How, I don't know. The only oddness I remember was the sky. It looked peculiar, a little too leaden; they've probably done something to it. But that wasn't it either. I don't know. A man simply senses these things. And once he does, the actual evidence begins to pile up so fast he hardly has time to collect and interpret it. That's what these notes are for. I've got to jot down certain things before they're forgotten and lost to us.

First of all—if it isn't already clear—I'm in a hoZpital. H-o-z-pital. That's right, Z.

I'm in the obZervation ward. O-b-z. Z again.

I can't possibly list all the zees connected with this case. Here and there I'll indicate the more subtle ones that might otherwise be missed, but I'll have to rely upon the reader to catch the more obvious ones. As I said, there's this time problem.

Back to this morning: I knew when Miss Z came toward my bed with her thermometer she was bringing the clue with her. And I knew that at the instant my eyes connected with her face, she'd present me with the first real signal. If you can understand that. It's fairly subtle, rather mysterious. Which is one of the problems, so many subtleties in this thing.

I couldn't look at her, not at first. I didn't dare. I had to arrange this awareness carefully in my mind and prepare a reaction to it. For instance, if I'd shown surprise, or fear, I'd have been finished. Instinctively I knew it was important to keep her from realizing I'd caught the signal. It's better if you see it, and get it, but don't let them know you've got it. Just play dumb. I could give a thousand reasons why this is the best way to play it, but I don't have time. Just take my word for it.

So. Finally I did look at her, my own face a carefully set blank. And of course Miss Z was looking at me. (Later, you'll appreciate the irony of this particular Z. It's not her real name. It's what I call her in my mind. Z for Zoe. Zoe means *life* in Greek. You'll see how bitter this irony gets.)

The minute she caught my eye, she opened her mouth and smiled, and there it was: her upper lip, plus a kind of, how can I describe it, a diagonal, almost invisible shadow formed perhaps by her tongue, and then her lower lip. Taken altogether they formed a perfect, a deliberate, a malicious Z.

Oh, she was so pleased with herself. It was written all over her face, the delight she took in her own exquisite cleverness, placing the Z in a smile. So easy to deny later if anyone accused her openly. No evidence to be caught with, you see. She wouldn't have dared put it in a note or say it out loud for witnesses to hear.

She was disappointed when I didn't lose control of myself. I felt like shuddering or screaming. But I didn't. I smiled right back. And without a Z, as if I hadn't caught the signal at all. This would give me about three minutes, while the thermometer was in my mouth, to think. I had to think. And fast.

She lingered by the bed, fussing with her charts, nearly falling over with nonchalance. I wanted to hit her.

"I've got an idea!" she said. "Why don't you shave today?" She spoke like some nitwit kindergarten teacher proposing a lovely game of mud pies in a bed of quicksand. "You have such a handsome face, but it's all hidden by those whiskers."

I said nothing. The thermometer was in my mouth. Miss Z only asks questions when your mouth is full.

"Suppose I just bring the razor," she said, "and put it on that table. Then if the mood strikes you, you can simply plug it in! How's that sound?"

(Is it necessary to point out that an electric raZor, *simply plugged in,* makes an absolutely distinct *zzzzzzz?*)

"Would you like that?" she said, the cruelty too deliberate to ignore.

I pointed to my mouth, as if the thermometer were my reason for not speaking. Thank heaven I'm used to living by my wits.

"All right then, meanie," she said playfully, *"don't* answer. But that's exactly what I'm going to do."

This is what evil is, I thought as she walked away from me, her rear end stiff and secretive. From a certain point of view, Miss Z is beautiful. Blond hair, high bosoms, dark eyelashes, red lips, the works. Everything where it's supposed to be and of the right proportions. The sort of beauty they throw together in those big super drugstores. And I'm certain that making love to her would be disastrous. Only an insane person would dare, or perhaps a drunk or someone brutally insensitive. When I first saw her, of course, I allowed such a prospect to move once, quickly, through my own imagination. It was horrible. I realized at once that her juices were pure acid. At the very instant of penetration, the male member disintegrates entirely, the testicles, too, and the scrotum simply hangs there forevermore, as empty and useless as a pauper's purse.

My mind, as I've already indicated, works brilliantly under fire. The more danger there is, the greater its agility. Now, for instance, even before the winds of Miss Z's exit had subsided in the room, the plan had formed itself with no real effort at all.

I knew I'd kill her. And what's more, I knew exactly how I'd go about it.

If these notes are going to do any good at all, I suppose they should include a few autobiographical touches.

I'm 46. I was a boy during the twenties, a young man during the depression, a soldier during World War II. One day, while killing time behind a clump of banana trees in a very pretty tropical place, I heard a ZZZZZ sound. There was an explosion. I was hurt. Not badly though. They made a big do over it but if you ask me the damage was extremely slight. However this is not my point. I'm not telling a war story here. I merely wish to note that during the zzzzzz that preceded that explosion I came to know something, something important. I gained (all in a flash and through no effort of my own) a certain view of life as it is lived in the American century. And since then my own life has been more or less dedicated, I say this modestly, to the gathering of data, evidence, etc., in support of that view. Only recently have I begun to understand what might be done with these materials, how *urgent* it is, in fact, that I do what I can to initiate some sort of movement to counter this direction that everything has taken in recent decades. It was only this morning—I'm ashamed to admit this—only this morning have I actually taken pen and paper to make these notes. And the horror of it is, there may not be time to finish!

But here goes:

Concentrate. This may require concentration. Think back to the twenties and thirties. Remember the sound of a car door closing. It went Ka-Kloonk. And the horn went Ow-*oo*-ga. Today's car door goes *glooozhe,* and the horn, difficult to spell, is actually a shrill, baritone *zzzzzzz.* And recall please how in those days one *klomp-klomped* up a stairway. Now one ascends in an elevator, *zzzzzzz.* The sound of men working used to be KLONG*ang.* My father was a blacksmith. KLONG*ang,* went his hammer as it touched the anvil. Now, however, a rivet gun, a drill, an electric saw, all go *dzzzzt dzzzt.*

This may sound trivial. It is. I am purposely starting with things that aren't what you'd call crucial. But note, please, the general *softening* of everything, the tendency toward Z sounds.

(A word to the fainthearted: I'm trying to do this gradually, tastefully. I'm trying not to offend. But I must warn you, the thing itself gets pretty hairy. Remember, please, I don't like it any better than you do.)

People, and not just the rich, used to live in fairly big rooms with high ceilings, and when they laughed and talked they'd go *ha-ha-ha* and *talk-talk-talk,* good and loud and real. Now, living in these little cardboard shelves with paper walls, and under ceilings they can reach up and touch (a man should never be able to touch his own ceiling without a ladder) the talk is nothing more than *bzzzzz, bzzzzz, bzzzzz.* And it is well known that nothing of importance or size can be said in a situation where voices cannot be raised. Whispering, which is all that can take place in these rooms, lends itself best to the telling of petty secrets and the bearing of false witness against one's neighbor.

Interruptions: Miss Z just came in for the thermometer. And of course she brought the razor. The hideous thing is lying not two feet from my head at this very moment. But that's all right, that's just fine. You will see in due course how the razor has become a part of my plan.

I can tell, by the way, that Miss Z suspects nothing. It delights me to realize the wicked bitch will be dead by teatime, sawdust spilling from her heart, betsy-wetsy-doll eyes rolling back in her drugstore head. Alas, I have no time to indulge myself with these pretty images. Back to the low ceilings.

It is important here to touch upon a related matter: while the rooms men live in are shrinking in size, men themselves are actually becoming larger. (Not bigger, please; larger.) There is a village in West Germany where the average height of a 14-year-old boy is six-foot-four. Similar figures exist throughout Europe and America. I have no time—and surely there's no need!—to suggest what will result when this size-of-man size-of-room ratio, already absurd, reaches its ultimate limits; the intelligent reader will have seized the picture without assistance. I must now proceed to the question of why people are growing to such ungainly proportions.

To put it bluntly, this food thing has gotten entirely out of hand.

They've found ways of creating fruits and vegetables without the sun, and the results of these techniques, to put it as simply as possible, create monsters. In appearance they are as perfect and handsome and enticing as Snow White's apple—a fairly lucky simile, for wasn't that article produced with poisons and gases in a dungeon under the palace, with no exposure whatever to true sunlight? As for fowl, there is no longer any night in the life of a chicken. It grows at a regulated speed in the light of a perpetual electronic sun, laying eggs of a grotesquely predictable size and quality. In death, this bird which has never seen sky or earth is interred in a block of ice and gift-wrapped by machines in see-through paper. Even on the table, the stuff looks splendid. And since the American century is the century of surfaces, people eat first with their eyes, seldom even noticing the absence of flavor and sweetness and mystery. The trouble is—at the risk of overworking the legend of Miss White and her fatal apple—the stuff induces in us a witch's sleep of death. Zzzzzz, Zzzzzz.

One note before we leave the kitchen: When was the last time anyone heard a cleaver going KLUNK, the *snap-snap* of a pea, the *whack* of a carrot being cut, or milk bottles going *klonk* against one another in an icebox that went *drip-drip*? In place of these, there is one endless deadly *zzzzzzz* of refrigeration and an occasional *dzzt* as some pretty-colored frozen falsehood hits boiling water —in the kitchen*ette*.

Enough has been said that the reader may have guessed what sort of place this is, this hospital. It's a place for the recalcitrant, for the few who refuse to succumb to Z. We reZist. And we are gathered up, one by one, and placed in these institutions for processing and ultimate dispoZal. We are slowly Z-ed away to nothing, or practically nothing.

For instance, the night before last, Mr. Highet reached the end of his processing. Yesterday morning, Miss Z carried him out in the palm of her hand.

I said, "What have you got there, nurse?" I knew, but I wondered what she'd say.

"What have I got *where*?" was her brilliant rejoinder.

"Oh, in the palm of your hand," I said casually.

"This?" She opened her plaster-of-paris fingers. "It's just a capsule."

Obviously they had Mr. Highet in this capsule. When they finally Z you out for good, it makes you very small in every way. You look like a bit of dust. Sometimes the orderly carries out the remains, hidden in a bucket of scrub-water or a dustpan. I've seen them hauled out of here every which way, in pillow cases, in bits of Kleenex, in water glasses, ashtrays, slop jars, bedpans. They don't care how: *get them out*, that's all that matters. But I will say this is the first time in memory of someone being hauled out in a capsule. Apparently, sensing I'd caught on to their other methods, they felt called upon really to tax their meager ingenuity.

"May I see it?" I said.

"*Why* on earth?"

"Oh, just curious."

She thought for a while. "Well, all right. Why not?" She lowered her palm. "See?"

The capsule was fairly large, and black as death. I wondered how she'd got him in there so quickly—although I had observed that these people are fairly good with their fingers.

"What kind of capsule is it?" I said.

"Vitamin," she answered quick as a wink.

"Oh, I see. Well, if it's a vitamin, why don't you swallow it?"

That got her. I felt her shuddering. I laughed. I don't blame her for loathing me. I *am* difficult. They're not used to my kind in here.

"I don't need it," she said. "I've had my vitamin today."

"Yes," I said, "I thought you had."

She smiled and began to leave.

I said, "Nurse?"

She stopped.

"Nurse, where is that gentleman today?" I pointed to the bed by the window.

"Mr. Highet? Why, he went home this morning."

"Oh? Well, isn't that curious, because I didn't see him leave."

"You mean you don't believe me, is that it?" she said. The same old smile: *come, kiddies, mud-pie time!*

"I didn't say that, I didn't say anything at all, I just said I didn't see him leave."

"Tell me," she said, "where do you think Mr. Highet is?"

I just looked at her. I'd already pressed the point too far and I knew it. She stopped smiling and something happened in her face that told me they were going to close in and finish me off next.

However, I didn't think *immediately*. I thought I'd have a few weeks or at least a few days. But then this morning, as I've already described, it became inescapably clear that they intend to get me tonight.

Intend.

I have a few intentions of my own, thanks.

The plan is simple, and foolproof. At first blush it may seem to constitute a complete reversal of my initial stand, but that's actually the genius of it: I will create the impression that I have ceased all resistance. (I take no credit for this strategy, it's an ancient one: give the enemy false confidence, it's as simple as that.)

When Miss Z returns to the ward, I intend to make a *Zzzzz* sound at her. I'll repeat this every time she passes my bed. This will give her the impression that I have accepted her signal from this morning, and therefore my fate.

Secondly, I'll shave. With a concerted effort of the will, this can be done without the *zzzzz* actually entering the brain. Shaving is important. To their kind of mind, it will seem to be the ultimate capitulation. The psychiatrist here has been prattling on vomitously for weeks now about the beard being a father imitation that will "fall away"—if you can stand the expression—"when the father within comes to birth." Understand please, he's deadly serious about all this tripe.

Thirdly, at just the right moment, probably late this afternoon, I'll place a bit of dust on the sheet and hide myself under the bed. Miss Z, finding the dust on her next tour of the wards, will assume my processing has concluded a few hours in advance of their calculations. And while she's gathering up my proxy for disposal, I'll seize her legs from under the bed. There'll be a brief struggle and in a matter of seconds she'll be dead from strangulation.

Reading over these notes, I realize I may seem somewhat overwrought, a bit too vexed by the more trivial aspects of this Z-situation: television, the constant electronic *bzzzzzz* of today's world, all the subtle new Zees the Bell System has been introducing into long-distance telephoning, etc. I've said too much, perhaps, and risked running out of time before I get to what is important: the zeeing of love.

My attitude in this connection was the *specific* reason for my being brought here in the first place. Therefore, even at the peril of allowing these notes to descend to the level of a woe that is merely personal, I'll deftly sketch in at least the rough outlines of my own situation.

To begin with, love has been done away with, damn near. I've been watching it happen since World War II. At first it seemed fairly gradual, but one should realize that the gradual, seen by some standards other than the purely optical, might indeed be quite appallingly rapid. The death of a rose for example cannot be observed by the naked eye but it takes place nonetheless overnight. And so it has been with love. People still prate and blab and sing about it a good deal, perhaps even more than ever, like homage to the dead; but the article itself is well-nigh gone from the world. And where did it go?

Like everything else of value, it's being Z-processed in a thousand insidious ways, but mostly it's being tranquilized out of existence.

The process is simple: Love is caring. Tranquilizers subdue, mute, deaden, the caring centers in the brain. That's all there is to it. A tranquilizer is a lobotomy in pill form. Or to say it more accurately, it is a soporific for the soul. *Zzzzz-zzzzz-zzzzz,* sleeps the soul. While love dies.

Why is this being done? First of all, it isn't love per se that's under attack. It's the trouble it brings. This American time of the world is a deadly efficient time. For instance, instead of using architecture to solve the housing problem, it seeks to solve the housing problem by destroying architecture. Why? Well, no one has ever succeeded in measuring or even naming the precise function of beauty. All that's known is the price of maintaining it and how much space it occupies. In our times these figures have been declared to be too great.

Love is in a similar fix. Its function, like that of an old Park Avenue mansion, eludes these tragic new mathematics. Love's measurable products, e.g., songs and babies, can be produced in quantity by quite other means. Therefore the trouble it brings, anxiety, the blues, jealousy, inconvenience, etc., is thought to be insupportable. A person simply turns off the telephone and munches little white pills until the danger is past and the troublemaker is dead in him. From a certain point of view, this works. One might even say it has worked so well that love on the contemporary landscape constitutes no more of a threat to the public safety than the buffalo. Nowadays neither is likely to be allowed to gather in sufficient force for a stampede. Both, for all practical purposes, both love and the buffalo, have had it.

Miss Z just came in.

I said, "*Bzzzzzz*," as per plan.

"Oh!" she said, "that's the sound a razor makes!" The bitch. I nodded.

"Does that mean you're going to shave for me?"

I nodded again, docile as a poodle. Miss Z smiled. She looked genuinely, profoundly relieved, like a junkie who's been promised a fix.

Evil evil evil.

I gritted my teeth and returned her smile. "*Zzzzzz*," I said.

"Uh-huh, and *zzzz zzzz zzzz*," she said. It's-the-loveliest-game was her attitude. "Would you like me to plug it in for you?"

I started to shake my head, but caught the gesture just in time to turn it into a nod.

She plugged in the razor and handed it to me. I waited for her to leave, but she just stood there watching.

She said "Wouldn't you like me to do it for you?" When things are going their way, they become unbelievably bold. But I had to say no this time, I just couldn't risk it.

Finally, she left the room, and I shaved. I'm absolutely certain the *Zzzz* of the razor did not really penetrate. I kept saying K-K-K-K-K-Kill, K-K-K-Kill over and over again the whole time, and I'm sure those good hard sounds counteracted the *Zzzz* almost entirely.

It will now be seen how certain events in my own life perfectly illustrate my thesis on the subject of love in the nineteen-sixties. I am here because I refused to allow my love to be demolished. Specifically, when my ex-wife refused to see me or even to answer the telephone, I broke into the apartment. I went to the roof and down the fire escape and kicked in the bedroom window. The place was *thick* with electronic rays. She was in the living room using the television, the air conditioner and the hair dryer *simultaneously!* But still she heard me enter and ran screaming down the halls. Busybody neighbors, roused momentarily from their *zzz*-slumbers, called the police. *Who* of course were lurking somewhere nearby in a squad car full of radio waves. I was apprehended.

My entrance into the apartment that night was in violation of something called a peace bond my wife had acquired in court some weeks earlier. She got it by claiming I tried to kill her.

Which wasn't the case at all. I was simply trying to awaken her, as she had fallen slowly, almost imperceptibly at first, into the clutches of this Z-thing.

The poor woman—Bennington, class of '48, formerly the world's most tiresome exponent of natural childbirth, and the only debutante in history to insist upon a bare-footed outdoor wedding—this woman was actually strangling in appliances by the time I discovered the Z-pills. There were quarrels. That is, *I* quarreled. She gulped pills. Couldn't have been more agreeable, went around with a perfectly asinine, beatific grin all the time, and I couldn't bear it. The simple fact was she was dying. I knew it and tried to save her and somehow in the process happened to leave a few little blue marks on her throat. Anyway, here I am.

(Just for one wild moment, in the interest of looking under every little pebble for truth, let's consider that I *was* trying to kill her that night. Isn't there something to be said for real death as opposed to living death? And isn't that precisely what Z amounts to? Has anyone, anywhere, ever postulated an even faintly valid reason for enduring a life from which love is gone forever? Is there anyone—I do not here address myself to the dying, which includes of course the virtually millions of Z-puppets who clutter the world—is there anyone among the living few who knows a way to continue the labor of breathing without at least some small hope that love might one day be revived in him? Of course not.)

Teatime approaches.

I found my proxy, my effigy, on the bathroom floor.

It's not the kind of dust I'd hoped for, a fine, fuzzy, gray little tumbleweed of the sort that gathers under beds. They don't seem to have that kind here; undoubtedly it reminds them of their sins. What I did find looks like a bit of mud from someone's shoe. But it'll do nicely. I've placed it in the middle of the bed and it looks rather peculiar there, this tiny fragment of clay against the white of the sheet.

I think perhaps it's the saddest thing I've ever seen.

But it's time now to get under the bed.

How nice this is. I had no idea I'd be able to write under here. Hospital beds are fairly high, so there's plenty of room. I'm lying on my stomach. It's not really comfortable, but it's cool and pleasant in other ways. I'm exhausted now. When I look up, I can see that peculiar sky out the window.

I wonder if it's really winter. They could easily have put that snow effect out there, any good stagehand could show them how. But then, why would they do that, how can it be to their advantage to make me think it's winter? I've been thinking so much today I can't quite piece everything together now. But I do hope the snow is real. It's in my head now and I don't want anything false in there. And then, too, real snow can have such peace in it. My mother, the foolish old dear, used to say it was torn up notes from God. She didn't say what was written on them. Or why He tore them up. Maybe if I knew I wouldn't be under this bed.

Funny, but I can't remember any more what I'm doing here. I only remember something about it being urgent.

I hear footsteps. A lot of them.

Oh, God!

THE
ASTRAL
BODY
OF A
U.S. MAIL
TRUCK

Note to the person who finds this important document upon my death. I, Mrs. Dorothy Fitzpatrick, urge you, in fact I beg you, please to send a copy of it to Duke University, the Extrasensory Perception Department they have there which I've read about. Another copy please to the Institute for Studies in Spiritualism in Long Beach, California. And if the finder has half a heart to understand with, upon finishing his or her perusal of this document, he or she will undoubtedly be pleased to see to it that a copy gets into the hands of my neighbor right here in Tampa, Mrs. Malvina Cheney, who lives catty-cornered across the street. I myself have severed all relations with this person, for reasons that will become self-evident upon further perusal.

Purpose. For all I know I am breaking new ground here, and wish to bequeath my tiny bit to the great storehouse of human knowledge on certain subjects, to wit:

It is known that dogs and cats and horses and such have ghosts as well as people. That is, they have definite spirit life after decease. Surely there is ample evidence on file in the above places on that score. Cases for instance where a person and her pet, like my former neighbor Mrs. V. and her dachshund, were killed simultaneously at the same time by a speeding auto in front of a fruit market on the Tamiami Trail. And not only did Mrs. V. make an appearance to loved ones after being thus jarred loose from her physical container, but also the little dog right along with her as well.

This is common enough I have no doubt, but now I wish to add to this body of knowledge the fact that even a machine can put in an astral appearance, under certain circumstances. In my own experience, to wit, a U.S. Mail Truck.

The record: I include here certain notes of an autobiographical nature for whatever they may be worth to students of the subject. I am a lady living alone at the age of forty-eight for the better part of two years since my husband passed away in a shrimp boat that sank in a gale off Key West, and am of sound mind. Although of course his passing left me distraught for some time thereafter which I do not consider in any way an abnormalcy. Particularly not since I was able to function fine right after his death, continuing to hostess at the Two Skippers Marine Grill and Yacht Club Lounge on Caroline Street, knowing it's best to keep right on going in a time of loss for otherwise the thing can get the best of you. Naturally I took off until the funeral was over, but was there at the old stand the very next day, and cheerful too, of which I am proud, not unduly.

But this is veering from my topic.

For reasons that have nothing to do with these notes, I saw fit to retire the following year at the age of forty-seven, and take it just plain easy for a change in my lovely white cottage on Front Street. Frankly, I am a great reader in matters of metaphysics, astrology and spiritualism, and saw fit to pursue these studies in earnest during the remaining years left to me.

I do not consider forty-seven *old* by a long shot, but it seemed to me I ought to begin to develop my inner life against the cold time of old age, so as not to become a sad elder citizen with nothing to fall back on at all. Possibly my younger years had not been spent too wisely according to the standards of the average person. That is, I did not jump into marriage and have a lot of kids, etc., but instead chose to have a good time for a little while, which went on well into my thirties. And so perhaps I, a childless lady, had some regrets on that score and wanted to do better with the rest of my years now that the Captain (my husband) had made the Big Change, leaving me on my own again.

It was in this frame of mind that I settled into my widowhood in the lovely white cottage on Front Street, living on income from the Two Skippers Marine Grill and Yacht Club Lounge, which half interest in it was left me by the Captain.

The truth is, I was not too miserable. I told myself he was at sea (which of course he was) on a voyage from which he would not return to me—but one day I would join him. That was the philosophical way I looked at it, and was therefore not too miserable at all.

I turned to feminine matters such as my little garden, and began to tend it in earnest. Each morning I got up at seven or so and drank coffee in the garden while fiddling with ferns and flowers and seeds and such. Then later, after a bit of toast and an egg, perhaps I'd study for an hour or two there in the shade of the banyan tree, study my astrology charts and just plain meditate into the flowers at times. Mornings in this part of the country have excessively blue skies, and our birds here are known to sing in abundance.

Thus everything went along reasonably splendid for the first year.

Mail is delivered in our neighborhood at about eleven-thirty A.M. The mailman (who I will call Sidney as a non-diplume—not that I think he'd be ashamed, but it is of no concern to anybody else's business) was a very nice vigorous man, fairly short and perhaps a smidgeon younger than myself, with a fine smile. He used to ride up every morning on this very cute type of three-wheeled truck they give the mailmen to use for their rounds here lately.

The way I'd know he was coming was as follows: I'd hear the motor from about two blocks away. It did not make a *VVvvrrrroooommm* sound like an ordinary car motor. I'd say it was more like a thousand putt-putts all jammed together into a very few seconds. At any rate it was just the proper sound for a fine little red white and blue truck to make, and after a while I noticed that just the mere sound of it made my heart go *putputputputput* each morning when I heard it.

All of which is not at all extraneous to the record, as students of these matters will soon see as more is revealed. For it was this kindrid sounding in my own bosom that tipped me off finally as to how I felt about Mr. Sidney Ritter. (This was in the *second* year after the death of the Captain, I might chance to repeat, certainly not the first.)

I received a good deal of mail in those days. I sent for literature for my studies, plus assorted magazines, and also wrote quite a few letters and received answers from people on these topics that interest me, namely, spiritualism, metaphysics, etc., as noted above. Therefore, Sidney always had something for me, it seemed.

He also customarily had a bill or a catalog or some trifle to deliver to my catty-cornered neighbor, Mrs. Malvina Cheney. This woman was always waiting for him each morning in front of her quite ugly green-and-yellow house. It was Sidney's next stop after my own tasteful white cottage.

It is my unpleasant duty to inject here, for the purpose of accuracy, a note on Mrs. Cheney's unfortunate character. The woman is a dangerous troublemaker of the first water. She seldom leaves her front porch (even gives herself henna packs there) for fear of missing something. Usually of course there are red henna splotches all over her unfortunate face. Several months were destined to pass before Malvina Cheney would present me with evidence to support my first hunch about her, namely, that she is of a very low order of human life and deserves our sympathy.

Now I intend not to beat around the bush at all. Students of these matters will understand.

Sidney Ritter and I started in having a love affair.

Note please that Sidney was not a married man, but a widower with three good-looking but ungrateful children. When his wife died, he went back to living with his mother, a dominating (Scorpio) creature who made his life miserable. All she ever had to say to him in the way of conversation was accusing him of various faults, etc. I see no reason to go into her character, but wish to give a picture of the pathetic home life of a gentleman whose children had been alienated from him by a dominating Scorpio.

Which explains, I believe, his lonesomeness for decent human company.

Sidney began to come around in the evenings, after first of all faithfully having supper at home for the sake of his kids even though I doubt they appreciated it. Then he would come and sit in my garden, sometimes sharing a can of beer or two with me at the most.

I don't know if two people make a simposium, but let me say right here that we had wonderful talks on all subjects, politics and love and exceedingly deep matters. And sometimes merely our own personal feelings. Out of all due respect for the Captain who was no kind of talker at all (although a fine and faithful husband in other respects) I believe Sidney's company was as excellent as any I'd ever enjoyed in my life.

Frankly, he thought the world of me as well.

"Dorothy," he said to me on that first evening, sitting in a wicker chair in my garden, "I have never taken you for just an ordinary woman with a good figure and blond hair, far from it." And then he confessed to me that even in the old days before he had the Front Street route, he used to see me now and then, crossing a street somewhere or hostessing at the Two Skippers, and admired me in a special way. He stated that I had "eyes with a capital E."

(Although I do have exceptionally large pale blue eyes, set wide apart which men like, he was undoubtedly making reference to the fact that I have second sight. For I was born with a veil.)

Let me state that I did not remember Sidney at all from those old days. First of all, I did not have the habit of looking around at other men while married to the Captain, not even when he was on a three-week trip at sea. (I have indicated that my younger years were not spent too wisely, but do not interpret this too hastily, as I have always been a one-man woman. That is, during the duration of all intimate associations, I have practiced strictest fidelity.) And second of all, a mailman looks very different out of uniform.

But it was this ability of Sidney's to look beneath the surface of a woman, to see not only the color of her eyes but some of her deepest feelings, that drew me to him from the start.

There is no need here to delve further into the extremely personal events of that night, the night he reported to me his fondness for my eyes. But let it be said that henceforward the sound of a U.S. Mail Truck was better music to me than even the finest blues record on the jukebox at the Two Skippers Marine Grill and Yacht Club Lounge on Caroline Street.

Late in the mornings from then on, whenever I heard the first faraway *putputputputput*, the effect on me was such that I was forced to cease whatever I was doing and catch my breath. At times I had to sit down altogether before regaining enough strength to go out and wait for him to turn the corner into Front Street.

(I think the government is to be profoundly saluted for giving out these little trucks, which make all the difference between night and day in the life of any mailman. For now, with all that power under him, he is like a gallant horseman on his daily rounds, instead of a beast of burden with a heavy pack on his back as in the old days, on foot. But this is veering.)

At the start of our association, Sidney always arranged to touch my fingers in a lingering way as he handed me my envelopes. And sometimes, in a whisper, he would communicate some sweet message of a personal nature. The two of us, like high school children in love, enjoyed greatly the pleasurable throes of our secret.

And then we became somewhat reckless.

Sidney took to coming back to the garden with me for a few minutes to have a cup of coffee. It seems we had forgotten altogether the hostile presence of Mrs. Malvina Cheney on the porch of her green-and-yellow, excessively tasteless house across the street.

Late in the summer, Sidney's mother went to the hospital for what would prove to be a nasty though not fatal operation, and for more than three weeks Sidney had to stay home every single evening to tend to his children. A neighbor woman looked after them in the daytime, but as is only proper, Sidney took over for himself in the evenings. Therefore, that August, we saw each other only at the brief two or three minute coffee sessions that Sidney could snatch from the government quite harmlessly each morning. And so it went, right into September.

On the first Tuesday of the month, it so happened there was a heavy rain going on at mail time. Certainly we could not sit in the garden, quite naturally, and so Sidney stepped into my living room.

It is only necessary to state here quite flatly that on this particular rainy morning, Sidney and I lost control of ourselves. (I'd like to add that this had never before taken place on government time. However, on that morning, it did.)

Up to this point, I had no concrete evidence on which to base my suspicion of the true depths of lowness of Malvina Cheney's nature. Previously, I had merely taken the view that she was coarse, and let it go at that.

But that rainy Tuesday morning, incredible as it may be to believe, Sidney stepped out of my front door, and there, *right on my porch,* stood this creature, dripping wet and carrying a closed umbrella.

"Don't you touch me!" she screamed. Naturally Sidney had not the slightest intention of touching that low person. On pain of death, he would not have touched her with her own closed umbrella, I might add. But she kept shouting at him, and making no sense whatever. "You're a public servant, do you hear me, and I want my mail! You're my employee, do you know that?"

Sidney tried to get past the woman, but she stood there blocking the steps and spilling out these thoughts from her very low-vibration mind, and saying, "Don't you dare touch me!"

It was hard to believe that such a nightmare was taking place right there on my own front porch in the rain. Sidney and I were both struck dumb with the horror of it.

"Don't you think the post office won't hear about this," she said. "I've known what was going on over here, for months now I've known all about it!"

Sidney was trembling understandably. He looked straight into my eyes, pleading with me for help. That did it. Knowing the high regard he had for my eyes, and seeing him look into them for guidance, my dander was up.

"Malvina Cheney," I said in a cold and frightening tone of voice. "You remove yourself from my front porch this precise second, or I'll tear you in half."

I am unable to report accurately what took place next. I do not believe I actually *handled* the woman, but somehow Sidney got past her. He flew down my front path and into his truck, Malvina Cheney right behind him broadcasting at the top of her voice. It was raining harder than ever. Poor Sidney was soaked to the bone. It looked like every front porch on the street had people on it now, mostly women, and they were all looking and listening to every foul word that came out of that mouth.

I stood on my porch and cried like an infant. Sidney had some trouble getting his motor started. He kept pumping and pumping with his foot. Somehow he got it going and went speeding away up the street at a terrible speed. Malvina Cheney went right on, marching up and down the sidewalk with her umbrella hoisted, her mouth going a mile a minute at its usual excessive volume.

I went back inside. For some reason I kept looking at the bed, at the crumpled pillow where Sidney's head had been. I remember this part very clearly. I was leaning on the doorway of the bedroom, telling myself that what I wanted most to do was to go over to the bed and take up that pillow and hold it next to my face. But I never made it to the pillow.

The accident took place then. It took place right on the corner of Front and Caroline Street. I heard it, the whole thing. Two different screeches of brakes, one of them Sidney's and the other an enormous moving van, and then the worst crashing sound I ever heard in my life.

Yes, I heard the whole thing very clearly. And I just kept looking at the pillow, wanted to go hold it, but unable to move.

The purpose of this record, as heretofore stated, is not to dwell upon my own mortal agony and such trivial emotions. These after all will pass, along with the body which is merely a dollar and a half worth of chemicals.

I intend to restrict myself to a record of the evidence pertaining to the activity of the spirit after it has stepped out of its material bonds.

The following morning, the Tampa *Sun-Times* carried a front-page story of the terrible wreck of the post office truck and the moving van. There were photographs printed with it. At the bottom of the article, it said the name of the funeral home where Sidney would be laid out.

Frankly, I laughed out loud. This may seem crusty, considering the three orphans. But having the knowledge I have acquired through my studies, the notion of death does not truly faze me at all. My only sad thought about Sidney was that he should have made the Big Change in such a violent smash-up. It seemed to me he deserved better than that, but these things alas do happen occasionally, even to very fine people when they have the misfortune of getting their paths crossed up with inferior vibrations of the sort we have on our street.

But I need not have worried for a minute. Because it turned out that Sidney himself was in fine fettle.

That morning, the morning after the crash, was fine and sunny. Of course I had not slept, for in such circumstances sleep is often withheld from a person. I was sitting in the big overstuffed chair in my living room where I had spent the night with Sidney's lovely crumpled pillow next to my face. And at eleven-forty, I heard, as usual, the most beautiful sound in the world, a faraway *putputput-putput*.

My emotions of that moment may have some pertinence to the record. Therefore I report that I experienced no surprise whatever, but merely a great wave of happiness, a more tremendous joy than anything I had ever experienced in my life. And I had not one doubt that the truck I heard was Sidney's and that he himself was the driver. People's driving is just like their voices or their handwriting. Nobody could ever imitate the way Sidney Ritter took a corner in that little truck. Of if they tried, they might fool Mrs. Cheney, but not a person so sensitively attuned to the sound as myself.

Next, as on many a morning in the past, I felt the same weakness in the stomach at the sound. I caught my breath and stepped out onto the porch into the sunlight. I am pleased to report that Mrs. Cheney was nowhere in sight. I walked up my little path and stood at the sidewalk, and soon, much closer than before, I heard the *putputput-putput,* and then I saw Sidney and the truck.

It was just as red white and blue as ever. If there was any change at all (and I would not *swear* to this detail), it seemed to me Sidney took that corner with even more style than I'd ever seen him do it before.

I watched him swerving zigzag up the street, stopping first on one side and then the other, until at last he reached my gate. Something told me Sidney did not want today to be different from any other day. Certainly he was not interested in a discussion of the previous day's misfortunes. He wanted to forget any reference to that altogether.

I said, Good morning, Mr. Ritter—in exactly my usual voice. And he said, G'morning, Mrs. Fitzpatrick. Then, just as on the first morning following the start of our intimate association, Sidney whispered to me, "No mail today, but I think you got my message."

Later that day a second uniformed man came by the house and put something in my mailbox. Of course the post office had to put on someone to replace Sidney Ritter.

But as far as I know I'm the only person on the block that gets two deliveries a day.

I have not seen this new man at all. And since I

am busy with my studies, I seldom see anyone, even Sidney. But I always hear his truck, and sometimes I hear it at night, too, *putputputputputput*-ing along on its zigzag way and swerving around in colossal style through all the streets of heaven.

My final suggestion, which it occurs to me the above facts may support, is this: that anything sufficiently loved in the time of its life may achieve immortality in the astral plane.

Additional note: Upon further reconsideration, I see no reason whatsoever for sending a copy of this record to Mrs. Malvina Cheney.

THE DAY
OF THE
SEVENTH
FIRE

Key West in 1936 was a dismal place. A bad hurricane had blown away the railroad, cutting off the island's one connection with the mainland. There were no jobs to speak of in that Depression year. Not much food either. A good fisherman always had something to set on his table, and you could get in line for sugar and grits and certain staples the Government was handing out; but many people had taken to eating grass and weeds, boiling the stuff with nothing to flavor it but a bird shot out of a tree with a BB gun. Some looked to Roosevelt for help and others said there'd be no letup at all: they blamed the bad times on a grand conjunction of certain heavenly bodies, claimed there was nothing to do but sit tight and wait for that movement of the stars.

There were those who believed in neither God nor Jupiter nor Roosevelt Himself and among this faction were a number who went berserk altogether: one old man took off all his clothes, ran into the swamps and died there a week later, stark-naked and alone; a middle-aged teacher surprised her students and colleagues one Monday morning by walking into the grade school dead-drunk, her hair freshly dyed the color of ripe tomatoes and twirling a loaded pistol round her forefinger; and so on. Nothing made sense any more.

Summer came and hot weather made things worse. There were reports of Peeping Toms and even rapes, countless minor burglaries and, by the end of September, seven cases of arson. A church, a hotel, and five residences had burned, most of them right to the ground. A firebug on the loose, along with all the other summer miseries, caused people to squint through suspicious eyes at old friends and neighbors and even at close relatives until, at the scene of the sixth fire, the maniac was apprehended.

Now, after a quarter of a century, the first six burnings of that evil summer have been pretty much forgotten on the island. But the seventh has not.

Even nowadays, on certain breezeless summer nights of talk and recollection, people huddled together on moonlit front porches of rickety old Bahama shacks will tell about that seventh fire and the events leading up to it. Many of the details seem petty or peculiar or a little absurd. But even the poorest listener of the bunch will not allow one word to go past his ear; for if there is one thing that can gladden the heart even more than a tale of love, it is one of revenge.

In those days there lived on the island, in a fine old house at the end of Cocoa Lane, a pair of old-maid sisters known as the Wiltons, Miss Erna and Miss Dolores, daughters of brave Captain Willy Wilton who was killed in the Spanish-American War.

Captain Willy left these ladies rich, just as rich as could be. Their lives were therefore a subject of more than routine interest in the town, and a body of common knowledge had grown up about them. The one tough and central fact, like the heartbeat of all else known about the Wiltons, was this: they were devoted to one another. They

got along like sweet teeth and taffy and that was all there
was to it.

Miss Erna, the taller, the elder, the stronger, was raw-
boned and had a long face; at seventy-six, she was agile
as an eagle scout.

It might be said of Miss Erna that she was beloved on
the Keys but not well-liked: people in general do not cot-
ton to stinginess, and stinginess was Miss Erna's main flaw.
Another factor sometimes operating in her disfavor has to
be touched upon briefly: a fondness for scatological words.
She often wrecked an entire conversation by maneuvering
to create a context in which to wedge one of them in (her
favorites were pee and poop) and a listener often found
himself so embarrassed he could only stand there wondering
what to do with his face.

But in spite of all, her loyal devotion to Miss Dolores
commanded the island's respect. For Miss Dolores was the
favorite of everyone, especially of children. She was kind-
hearted, plump and pretty, an excellent smiler. At seventy-
one she had eaten herself into the shape of a dumpling,
but still she was a dashing thing to look at: painted her
face, put bluing in her hair, and wore a black patch over
her left eye. (No outsider knew for certain, but the patch
was said to hide an enormous brown wart.)

All this charm, quite sufficient in itself, was further en-
riched by a smooth tongue and a keen and original sense
of justice. These gifts sustained her in a brief political
career: in 1924, ran for mayor on her own ticket, Children's
Suffrage, won seventeen votes on a platform that called
for a lowering of the voting age to seven; in 1926, decry-
ing the Movie Matinee Situation—slogan: *Saturdays Are
Too Far Apart!*—proposed all Wednesdays be declared
legal holidays, claimed to have in her possession letters of

support from Mary Pickford and the Pope, was defeated
again; in 1928, after a brief flurry in the primaries, was
dissuaded from running again by certain constituents who
had since graduated from grammar school; finally, declar-
ing that children as a pressure group cannot properly support a politician—"You grow too fast and before my very
eyes become the opposition!"—retired from the political
arena.

Some believed Miss Dolores's wart had been the sole
reason for which so splendid a creature had never married. Others claimed she had chosen to remain a spinster
because no man alive would wait on her hand and foot
as Miss Erna did.

The elder of the Wiltons was always seen offering her
arm to Miss Dolores at street corners. She was the carrier
of parcels, the keeper of books, the lighter of lamps, the
leader of the way. And it was her hand, the big, red-
knuckled hand of Miss Erna, that carried Miss Dolores's
hot-water bottles, emptied the slop jars, massaged away
her headaches, and fanned the air for her at all hot-weather
funerals.

Miss Dolores loved food; therefore the sisters ate
good. Their tastes ran to poultry and fish, goat cheese and
chocolate candy. They used cigarettes (Miss Erna blew
perfect smoke rings) and rum in moderate quantities (a
gallon of good Cuban stuff would last them six months).
And Miss Dolores even managed to get hold of enough
mad money so that she always had a twenty-five-cent piece
to slip into the hand of a child or a poor person.

But still it was true, as any shopkeeper or tradesman
would tell you, that in spite of these indulgences, her
sister Erna was far from being a spendthrift. No house

painter now living on the island could remember earning so much as a dollar on her property. If the house itself had not been sturdy, made of ironwood and teak, it surely would have gone to ruin along with the iron gates out front, which were rusty and had for years hung useless in a half-open position. The sisters kept no servants at all, not even a yard-man. The Captain's beautiful garden had long since gone to jungle and become a mating place for spiders and mos-quitoes and snakes. Certainly such a state of affairs can be attributed only to a terrible kind of parsimony in a rich old woman.

But since this defect, critical as it was, never seemed to show itself in Miss Erna's behavior toward her beloved Dolores, anyone would have sworn that all the demons of hell might break loose in Key West without marring even the surface of their profound compatability.

Until 1936 came along.

And then, perhaps inevitably, Miss Erna's selfish streak and the scandalous decline of that house on Cocoa Lane did at last set Miss Dolores's teeth on edge.

Earliest evidence of the rupture was gathered by Mrs. Emory P. Badin, the sisters' closest neighbor on the Lane. One morning in June, standing against a high board fence near the Wilton outhouse, she overheard a certain private conversation:

Miss Dolores wanted to move. Wanted to move into one of the little cottages the Captain had left them, one that had always been her special favorite, a bright, airy place with a tiny garden facing the water on Garrison Bight. The issue itself was innocent enough, but the tone of the quarrel aroused considerable alarm.

"I'm warning you, sister," Miss Dolores had said, "last

night I had an insight sharp as an ax, so take your choice: either we move out of this house, or something dreadful befalls us!"

"Something dreadful?" croaked Miss Erna.

"Oh, Lord knows what! The place'll burn up, or we'll be eaten alive by rats. Or murdered in our sleep. How would I know? The point is, we've got to move into that cottage on the Bight. I want to start in raising parakeets and flowers, and hang yellow curtains at the windows, and . . ."

"Yellow curtains, parakeets? Dear girl," said the older woman, "make sense!"

"I am fed up with broken shutters and hideous, scampering little feet in the night. I say we move, move this summer, or die some horrible death. Now that's straight from m'guardian angel, and you can take it or leave it."

(Miss Dolores did have a reputation for prognostication: if ever she stopped you on the street and said *Something fascinating is in store for you,* sure as shooting you would break an arm or win money on the Cuban lottery.)

But Miss Erna was unimpressed. "I never heard such fooltalk," she declared. "Move out of Papa's house? Why, Dolores Wilton, I'd as soon run naked down Duval Street and . . ."

(Oh yes, can just *hear* it, the neighbors said: that foul tongue on her!)

"I don't wish to hurt your feelings, Sister, but I can only assume you begrudge me the money it would cost to make the move."

Miss Erna clapped one hand over her own mouth, as if to hold back a hemorrhage; for this thrust, like truth, went straight to the heart of the old woman. Mrs. Emory

P. Badin claimed she heard a high, sad, moaning sound from the elder of the Wiltons, and then: "*Et tu, Brute?*"

Key Westers, sensitive to omens that summer, shook their heads. "Tch-tch, even the Wiltons have taken to scrapping—and that's *bad* news!"

On still another June morning, the younger of the ladies was seen running down Caroline Street, long blue hair undone, wind billowing her gone-with-the-wind skirt, and crying to beat the band. She had even forgotten her eye patch.

A moment later, long-legged Miss Erna in hot pursuit emerged from Cocoa Lane, easily overtook her sister and led her back home. But not before several neighbors had caught the gist of the quarrel. Mrs. Emory P. Badin heard Miss Dolores call her sister a miser. This brought gasps of disbelief, but the truth of it seemed to be shored up by Mrs. Jesús Ramirez, who quoted something even worse from Miss Dolores: "I just pray that firebug burns *our* place down before they catch him!"

For two weeks the sisters were not seen in the streets at all. This aroused much speculation. Some guesses were mild: "Oh, Miss Erna'll step out for them rents come first of the month, you'll see." On the other end of the spectrum was the theory that they'd murdered one another. But only certain girl children, who love nothing so much as the thought of bloodshed, had any real faith in the notion.

One Saturday morning two such creatures, little flowers of the fifth grade, stopped out front of the place, and one of them said, "I always sniff when I come by here lately." Her friend asked what for and she said, "Oh, to see if the Wiltons are dead yet, that's all."

At that moment, a light, fairy-queen voice from behind

the aralia hedge said, "No, they're not, dear." And Miss Dolores appeared before them.

The girls froze in their tracks.

Miss Dolores said, "Now can't you understand that just that kind of behavior gives a bad reputation to *all* children? Where do you think prejudice *starts?*" She smiled benignly, gave them each a quarter, and dismissed them. "Jane Withers is at the Palace; go there at *once* and learn sweetness!"

That afternoon the Wiltons were seen together rent-collecting and dime-store shopping as usual. (It turned out that Miss Erna'd had a touch of the flu.) People said the old woman appeared skinny with worry that day; and she was especially solicitous of her baby sister's comfort—even ordered the floorwalker at Woolworth's to bring out a stool for her to rest on.

Miss Dolores accepted the stool with grace, but the salesgirls, gathering round for their usual chat, thought she seemed unhappy, preoccupied; even her famous smile was lackluster.

She said, "Now, girls,"—many of them had been her followers in the old Children's Suffrage movement—"how many of you would have guessed that your leader would one day become a peculiar old woman living in a dilapidated house where children pass by each morning—and sniff to see if she's dead yet? Just raise your hands!"

Silence fell.

Miss Erna, pretending to be busy at the hardware counter, looked as guilty as a caught thief.

A certain event took place the following evening that put the fear of God into Miss Erna Wilton. The next morning she took Miss Dolores by the hand and together they marched into the sheriff's office where the entire story was repeated in detail:

Miss Erna had been clearing the supper dishes that night when a piercing scream issued from Miss Dolores's bedroom. She grabbed a frying pan in one hand, a bread knife in the other, and thus armed, flew to her sister's side.

She found Miss Dolores seated on her bed in an attitude of horror, hands crossed over her bosom, eyes closed, her breath coming in short gasps. Miss Erna questioned her, but she seemed unable to answer or even to hear. At length, she pointed toward the open window. Miss Erna, swallowing her own fear, went to the window and shouted in her most intimidating voice, *"Who is it? Who's out there?"*

She stood there for a long moment, studying the darkness. "I see you, Mr. Evil," she bluffed; and then, with candy-coated malevolence, "Please don't go 'way. I got a big jagged bread knife here, and I'm just dyin' for a chance to stick it in your gizzard. You hear me out there?"

After a moment in which there was no sound at all from the garden, Miss Erna moved to her sister's side and placed her arm about her shoulder. "What was it, little baby? Tell Erna what you saw at the window."

Miss Dolores made much of her inability to speak; and then she whispered, "It was the same one, been here a time or two before. I just didn't want to frighten you is all."

"Who?" said Miss Erna. "What're you saying, girl?"

Miss Dolores fanned out her fingers, and her right eye opened wide. "A man!" she said. "It seems like every time I go to close the shutters, he's waiting there for me with some ghastly fever in his eyes."

The sheriff promised to keep a sharp eye on Cocoa Lane, but Miss Erna wanted every assurance she could get. Key West that summer had already seen a number of unsavory goings-on, and she was determined her pretty sister would not be among the victims.

That afternoon the Wiltons were seen in Thompson's Hardware on Caroline Street making a purchase of two large cowbells. On the way home, they stopped at each house on Cocoa Lane and told their story.

"If you'll excuse me for stating my honest opinion," said Miss Dolores in several of her neighbors' parlors, "I think it's just some poor lonesome wretch that likes to watch ladies take their clothes off. A peeper? Isn't that what they call such persons? And of course that old house is *perfect* for them, set off all alone with a big yard around it and plenty of bushes to hide in. The shutters are all nicely broken up, too, so they can get a real good eyeful, but I doubt they's any real *danger*."

All the women protested that there was very grave danger indeed! Miss Dolores rather enjoyed the proceedings. At each house her story changed slightly. She seemed to have learned that the less she made of the whole thing, the more terrifying its effect upon her listeners. By the time the Wiltons arrived at the home of Mr. and Mrs. Emory P. Badin, Miss Dolores was in high spirits, chattering away gaily about how trivial the whole thing seemed to *her*.

Poor Miss Erna was more alarmed than ever.

By the end of the afternoon she had exacted promises from every man on the lane: when they heard the bells clanging (and she took the bells out of her bag at each house and gave a few sample clangs) they were to come a-running with shotguns and knives and big sticks, whatever weapons they could find.

On that very night, at a few minutes after ten, the first alarm was sounded; the Wiltons were calling for help.

Men came running down the lane in all states of disarray: clothed, semiclothed, some in pajamas, others in robes. Miss Erna gave orders from the kitchen porch: "Emory P. Badin, you search the stable. No, wait; I'd better send somebody with you. Juan, you go with Emory. Mr. Fisher and Nat Spatafora, the outhouse. I'd come with you, men, but I got to stay with sister. . . Jesús Ramirez, you take that stick and poke around behind my pandanus bushes."

In a few minutes the search was over.

No peeper, no prowler of any kind, was apprehended.

One by one and in twos, the men—nine of them all together—filed in through the kitchen porch to discuss the event with Miss Erna. Various views were exchanged and strategies proposed against future emergencies; and then talk got around to other summer happenings. One man told a rape story and Miss Erna was fit to be tied. She paced and swore and went to the window shouting threats and imprecations into the dark. The men found her anger awesome; and while they were enjoying the spectacle of it, another figure appeared in the door of the back hall and gradually drew all of their attention.

Miss Dolores stood there, smiling and calm—and wearing a new, emerald-green patch over her left eye. She was in full makeup, her blue hair carefully arranged in big, loose, upswept curls, and dressed in her best satin robe, a lovely dark blue thing that clung to her plump body like light and shadow on a nude. The men stared as she greeted them one by one, like a grand hostess at an impromptu party. And then she suggested that her sister might choose to reward their bravery with a thimbleful of rum.

Miss Erna brought out the jug and liberal quantities of the stuff were poured into glasses. Some of the men laid their weapons on the floor, and soon they were all sitting about in the great old kitchen, drinking and talking. This went on until long past midnight. Tales were told of the old days on the island, tales of wreckers and pirates, of ghosts and Chinese slaves; and some of the new legends of this very summer were reviewed and enlarged upon. The truth was told and lies were told; and each man contributed and each man believed, or seemed to. It was better than any party, Miss Dolores declared: more urgent, more exciting. Each man was at his best; for having responded to the ladies' bell of alarm he felt himself brave. And Miss Dolores, surrounded by a posse so fine and gallant, felt stirrings within herself that had been unfelt (but not forgotten) for a long, long time.

Miss Erna next morning at breakfast let it be known that she herself had not enjoyed the proceedings one iota, said the men had left a "certain odor" in the kitchen that would take days to get rid of. Miss Dolores laughed at this in a way that made the old woman fierce with anger. She rebuked Miss Dolores for appearing in such a "preposterous getup" the night before, and made a number of sharp comments on her behavior in general. But Miss Dolores, for some dark and worrisome reason, was imperturbable. She spent the day happily making new eye patches in a whole rainbow variety of colors.

And that night at about nine-thirty, the urgent *clang-*

clang-clang of cowbells was heard once again through the neighborhood of Cocoa Lane.

As the summer wore on, there were more and more of these unfruitful searches through the acre of jungle that surrounded the Wilton house. But the procedure became less and less partylike until at last it had achieved a kind of ceremonial dullness; fewer and fewer of the men responded to the clanging of the bells. Finally, on one sad Tuesday night toward the end of July, only one man roused himself; a Cuban gentleman named Juan who was so decrepit with age that any prowler worth his salt could have made mincemeat of him with just one arm and no weapon at all.

Nor had the atmosphere inside the Wilton house undergone any improvement: Miss Erna had begun to suspect that the peeper had been invented by Miss Dolores for the sole purpose of deviling her. One morning she even hinted aloud at this possibility.

"Damn funny, isn't it," she said, "how this bozo never shows his face to *me?*"

Miss Dolores considered this with a judicial frown; and then she said, "I can think of *one* explanation. Maybe he's not there at all. Perhaps I've lost m'mind and gone *se*-nile."

One evening early in August, the island's sixth great fire of the summer took place: the splendid old Cunningham home on Eaton Street. This event drew a large crowd. Even the Wiltons, who rarely set foot outside after dark, managed to get there while the blaze was still high, accompanied by several of their Cocoa Lane neighbors. Later they would be able to claim they'd actually seen the roof of the place cave in. It was a magnificent and terrible sight. Women wept and trembled and their men stood by sober and silent while firemen poked at the catastrophe with tiny, ineffectual streams of water; the best they could hope for was to keep the thing from spreading through the neighborhood.

The most sensational feature of the spectacle on Eaton Street was the apprehension of the firebug.

This was a tall and spindly, curiously sweet-faced boy of twenty who had been seen watching several of the earlier burnings that summer. Word got around that he was vagrant in the town, had wandered in some months earlier from the Carolinas. On this night, under questioning by the sheriff, he admitted setting all six fires. As the young criminal was being handcuffed, a confused smile played on his mouth: it was as if some colossal joke had gone seriously awry and he was trying to remember what had happened to spoil it.

Miss Dolores, who had maneuvered her way into listening range, came forward as the boy was being carted off. She laid a firm forefinger on the sheriff's heart. "Be gentle with him," she said, "and you may learn something about purity." The sheriff said, "Oh sure, Miss Dolores, we'll just coddle him to death." Miss Dolores seemed pleased with this answer. "It's all right," she told her neighbors, "I've interceded."

A little later, she collared one of the Cunninghams, a fat and weeping girl of fourteen. "Now, Sadie, listen to Miss Dolores," she said. "Tell your grandmother this: when the new house is ready, I'm presenting her with yellow curtains throughout—just the kind I'm going to have." The little girl stopped crying. She looked at the old woman and said, "What?" Miss Dolores cupped a gentle hand over the girl's mouth. "No, no!" she said. "I insist! It's the least I can do; yellow is the color of sunshine."

Then she continued moving about in the crowd gathering and disseminating bits of information: the Cunninghams had got out of the place in time and no one was harmed; a servant had risked his life to save an armful of Kewpie dolls and souvenir ashtrays while forty thousand in cash had gone up in smoke; a cat was thought to be trapped in the attic; later, the cat was reported safe and sound in the arms of an Episcopalian altar boy; and there developed a controversy over whether or not it was the same animal at all, and whether or not the altar boy was Episcopalian; and so forth. These items she collected and reported faithfully to her sister.

Miss Erna was less impressed with these details than with the blaze itself. She frowned and stared and murmured about "judgments" and the "anger of God." And then, just when the worst of it seemed to be over, something took place that struck Miss Erna far more profoundly even than the fire itself.

She saw, standing some five yards from herself and her sister, a peculiar-looking little man of some forty-odd years, staring at Miss Dolores—staring with the wide-eyed audacity of a child, but with none of a child's innocence. And then the man caught Miss Dolores's eye; caught it, yes; and what was more appalling, he held it, held it for a long nightmare moment in which that lady lifted the rose-colored patch over her left eye and returned the stare with such intense concentration that a kind of spell seemed to have been placed upon her mind.

Perhaps this bewitchment even extended itself to Miss Erna, for the older woman was so immobilized by her own fascination with these locked eyes that she was unable to speak until the moment had ended. The man disappeared into the crowd before Miss Erna could manage to begin her questioning:

"*What was that? Who was that man?*"

She squeezed Miss Dolores's arm, and would have repeated the question; but suddenly the reason for her own terror had arranged itself in words, and she was able instead to supply an answer. "It was him," she declared in a furious whisper. "It was him at your window!"

Miss Dolores was scared stiff. "Oh sister, oh sister!" She murmured these words over and over again like an incantation against the spell of her own fear. And she pressed herself close to Erna Wilton, hiding herself in the old woman's anger and indignation.

Later that night, Miss Erna, carrying a kerosene lamp, a shotgun and an old porcelain slop jar, led the way upstairs to the room above Miss Dolores's. This had been their father's bedroom, and for many decades no one had slept in it.

The old lady, exhilarated by danger, was more agile than ever: moved like a young man, carried her shotgun like one, and her voice had deepened half an octave. "Might as well throw out them cowbells altogether. No man alive any more is got guts enough to do his duty. But here's an old maid that has, by God! Oh, I'm dyin' to get a potshot at that son-of-a-seacook."

Her plan was this: Miss Dolores would sleep safely in Captain Willy's old bed, while she herself stood watch at the darkened window, directly above her sister's first-floor bedroom. A lamp left burning down there would lure the wicked prowler into target range, and then, *"Pow"*—she'd "pin his guts to the mahogany tree!"

"Oh, isn't it a pity?" Miss Dolores whimpered as her sister spread fresh linen on the bed. "Isn't it a pity we don't just check into the La Concha Hotel for a few days until we could get the little cottage ready? Isn't it a pity we're so cussedly stubborn we have to stay on in this old death-trap till we're carried out by the undertaker?"

Miss Erna gave no sign of having heard this talk at all. "Quit chattering, babylove, and hop in."

Miss Dolores lay flat on her back and pulled the covers up to her chin. "Poor old God," she said, "tries so hard to warn us; sends His angels to whisper in our ears. And we just never ever listen till finally He has to scream His lungs out and *hit us on the head!*"

Miss Erna took her place on a straight-backed chair next to the window. "I'm not sure whether to capture him and take him in—or just kill him outright!"

"Sister," said Miss Dolores, "may I ask when you plan to sleep, or have you given that up altogether?"

"Oh, in daylight's plenty of time for sleep. A little catnap now and then, just enough to keep m'eyes sharp."

"Well, I'd like to ask a favor. Tonight, while you're setting there fishing around for topics to think about, won't you give a little study to how sweet it could be, the two of us living in that white cottage on the water?"

Miss Erna was busy with her own thoughts, tales she'd heard of the island's earlier days, in which proud and gallant men like her father and Grandfather Wilton had protected their women and their young against every manner of nuisance from wild Indians to drunken pirates.

"Some people don't shoot to kill," she said aloud, "they

shoot to maim. That might be something to consider." Then she raised the gun to her eye and drew a bead on the moon, just for practice. "Mr. Evil, you think you run this world. Well, you know what Miss Erna says to that? Miss Erna says *tut-tut!*"

Erna Wilton got through that first night just fine. The second night was all right, too. She was proud of her ability to remain awake and alert with nothing to look at but the moonlit jungle under the window, nothing to listen to but the occasional scurrying sounds of wild things that had come to live there, raccoons and birds and homeless cats.

But on the third night she began to feel imprisoned by the whole damn mess. It didn't look like there'd ever be any prowler to shoot at. And yet she'd told it all over town, vowed everywhere that Miss Erna Wilton would not again close her eyes after dark until she'd nailed her man with a bullet. The poor woman was hemmed in on all sides: by the night, by the endless boredom of waiting, and by her own pride.

The next morning she was irritable. Her daytime naps in the humid and motionless summer air failed to restore her energies. Miss Dolores offered to fan her, but she was too stubborn to allow it. By the end of the week, a terrible melancholy had descended upon her.

Miss Dolores grew worried: her sister was not even irritable any more. She simply wasn't *there*, seemed no longer to see or hear or even feel. Miss Dolores herself developed a dreadful new fear: what if she should awaken one morning to find her sister slumped dead over the windowsill from heart failure or fatigue? She even went so far as to suggest calling in a doctor: "A soldier has to look after his health, doesn't he?" But Miss Erna answered this with such a savage snarl of contempt that it seemed best to drop the matter.

At length, Miss Dolores became so concerned that she no longer said her bedtime prayers lying down but knelt right on the bare hardwood floor. Nor did she continue to beg for the little white cottage with yellow curtains. "Just please keep us from getting *too* peculiar," she implored. "That's all."

By the end of the second week, Miss Erna had passed through melancholy into a state of angry despair that had about it some of the qualities of actual madness. She had taken to mumbling through the night, speaking her thoughts aloud. And Miss Dolores, resting none too soundly herself, heard some of these thoughts and more than once they'd sent a chill all through her bloodstream.

One night, for instance, Miss Dolores awakened to find her sister sitting on the edge of the bed talking at a salesman's pace about some kind of a "plan" that made no sense at all. The gist of it was that they run away to Chicago together "before Papa gets back."

Oh God, thought Miss Dolores, *Sister's mind has come loose at the hinges!* Miss Erna seemed to think the Captain was away on a long trip, that before leaving he had assigned to her the task of protecting the place; and somehow she had come to believe this was all part of some freakish stratagem he had devised to trap her on the property forever.

"He hates this place worse'n we do; else why is he always going off on trips to get away from it?"

"Erna?" Miss Dolores questioned softly. "Do you hate this house, too?"

"Like devils and snakes, I hate it. Like poison and death and big, hairy spiders."

Miss Dolores was so taken aback at this admission that for a moment she failed to consider that it had been spoken by an old lady almost deranged from sleeplessness and exhaustion. "Well, since you feel so strongly," she said, seizing her opportunity, "I wouldn't mind if we just moved out altogether! Who knows but what we might even find a little cottage somewhere! A white one would be nice! On the water! . . . Now let's just put our heads together and *think!*"

At this point, however, Miss Erna's conversation went from the strange to the incoherent, and then petered out altogether. The next morning at breakfast when Miss Dolores broached the subject, the old woman insisted it was Miss Dolores who was given to having nightmares, not herself.

And on the Friday night, Miss Dolores awakened just after midnight in time to hear this fearsome extension of that same nightmare conversation: "When Papa comes home, I'm gonna kill him."

Miss Dolores sat up in bed, goose-pimpled with fright. When she could use her voice, she said, "You what?"

"Gonna kill him," Erna said.

"But you know you love our papa!" Miss Dolores said.

"Then how come him to leave us alone like this?"

Miss Dolores forced her own mind back some forty-odd years. "Erna, honey, our papa has gone to fight the Spanish. Teddy Roosevelt has picked all his bravest men to go and help the Cubans. Aren't you proud enough to burst?" And then, to the heavens, she added, "Help me, sweet Jesus."

Miss Dolores got out of bed and went barefooted to the window. She placed her arm around Miss Erna's shoulder, squeezed her gently and looked into her eyes. "Our papa got killed, honey. Don't you remember the lovely memorial parade?"

Then a perplexing thing happened. Miss Erna looked at her and said, "Why of course I remember, precious! Is my little sweet having bad dreams again?"

"Me?" said Miss Dolores.

Miss Erna got to her feet. "Come on, let me tuck you in." Miss Dolores was confused. She climbed into bed, permitted her sister to stroke her brow for a few moments, and made no further reference to their eerie conversation.

When she had closed her eyes for what seemed no longer than a few seconds, a sudden racket at the window brought her rapidly to a sitting position.

"*Haaaaiee!*" shouted Erna Wilton. Then the shotgun crashed like thunder, followed by another Indian-like war cry.

Miss Dolores screamed and pulled the sheet up over her eyes.

"It's jammed, goddammit, it's jammed!" mumbled Erna Wilton. Holding the shotgun like a big stick, she took quick aim and threw the weapon itself. And then she let fly with some of the most sinful language she knew, hurling the ugly words out the window like big rocks. "He's tripped and fell; I believe I've winged the dirty devil! Gimme that slop jar, I'll finish him off!"

"And then I grabbed up the slop jar," she said next day, telling the story, it seemed to Miss Dolores, for the hundredth time. At this moment, which was early in the afternoon, the sisters were standing at the notions counter at Woolworth's surrounded by their audience of salesgirls.

"I held it just as dainty as you please, right by the handles, like so"—all this with gestures—"and I said to him, 'Mr. Tom, you down there, Mr. Peeping Tom, can I have your attention? I got something here with your name on it. I got a potful of pee for you. Don't go 'way!' And then I let her fly."

"Did you hit him?" one of her listeners asked.

"Well now, honey," said Miss Erna, rolling the moment around on her tongue like a swallow of cream, "what would be your guess? Would you say I hit him, or would you say I missed?"

"What I mean, did you *kill* him?"

"Naw. What I want to do that for?" Miss Erna had all the modesty of a boxer being interviewed after a first-round knockout. "I was only out to do him a little damage is all."

Miss Dolores was annoyed. At noon, she and her sister had set forth from Cocoa Lane to do some shopping. At each store, Miss Erna told her story of the night before. Miss Dolores had begun by nodding agreement to each detail. ("Oh yes, saw the entire thing with m'own eyes.") But as the tale grew, and Miss Erna's language became more and more explicit, her attention began to wander. She was bored and embarrassed. ("Erna Wilton, you're behaving something awful, saying pee in front of men. I warn you, quit!")

But Miss Erna would not quit, and her punishment was this: while they were standing there at Woolworth's, Miss Dolores, having got hold of about forty dollars in rent money, slipped away from the old woman altogether.

More than fifteen minutes had elapsed before Miss Erna, deeply engaged in telling her story all over again to the janitor, even noticed her sister was missing.

The hunt started at the Palace Theater. Miss Erna checked her sister's regular seat (back row on the left-hand aisle), the ladies' room and the candy counter. Then she went up and down Duval Street asking everyone she knew if they'd seen Miss Dolores. Clues gathered in this way indicated there had been an extensive shopping spree, but no one knew where to find the missing woman.

Miss Erna grew frantic. She began giving out a description to perfect strangers: "Pretty little thing? Gold patch on her eye? About so high? Are you sure? Now *think!*"

At one point, when the search had been going on for more than two hours, Miss Erna became aware that dark clouds had moved in over the island. She took this as a sign that life would never again be quite the same for either of them, not after today. And this thought filled her heart with a dreadful foreboding: "Oh, what if I never find her again?"

And then the old lady found herself standing in, of all places, a saloon, tapping on the counter with a fifty-cent piece. The bartender set a shot glass full of rum before her. Miss Erna picked it up, raised it toward the ceiling, closed her eyes and made a wish: *Come on now, You give her back to me, hear?* She swallowed the rum, left a ten-cent tip for the bartender (believing that God upon occasion had been known to accept bribes) and hurried back into the street.

Her glance fell once more on a marquee of the Palace Theater:

ELEANOR POWELL IN
BORN TO DANCE

Suddenly Miss Erna knew that her sister was indeed hiding somewhere in that movie house; the shrewd little creature had no doubt avoided her usual seat on purpose, just to throw her off the scent.

The usher, assisting Erna Wilton with his flashlight, found Miss Dolores way down in front eating a box of chocolates. Most of the money was gone. She'd given some of it away and had made a few purchases: a bolt of yellow chintz, a box of Whitman's Samplers, and a life-time supply of Tangee Red-Red. Miss Dolores made no excuses. Her only comment in fact as they passed through the lobby pertained to the quality of the candy: "The bottom layer is *never* as good as the top!" And Miss Erna, giddy with relief, was in no mood to scold. She chose instead to admire each purchase, and it was then she proposed a fish supper in the fanciest restaurant in town.

Before the sun had set, word got around on Duval Street that Miss Erna Wilton had not only shot somebody the night before, but was, at that very moment, sitting with her sister in Diego's Sea Food Palace at a table right next to the window, drinking rum like a sailor on payday.

Nor was this too far from the truth.

For at ten minutes after seven, when the sheriff arrived at Diego's to tell the sisters their house had just burned to the ground and a man with a bandaged thigh had been apprehended on the spot and charged with arson, Miss Erna gaily announced that it'd take more than a few flames to spoil her day—and went right on blowing smoke rings for the benefit of anyone who chose to watch.

Miss Dolores, however, did frown. But only for a moment. And then she filled their glasses and said she thought it'd be wasteful to buy another sewing machine: why not just hire a seamstress to make up the lovely new curtains?

LAUGHS,
ETC.

Tom, don't you think I should tell Ceil and Harry about Friday night? Well, *I* do.

It was truly one of those I mean like (quote) great nights (underscore). And it came about with no help whatever, it just took place. That's East Village, I mean its not the East Seventies. Things can still happen here, thank God we moved.

To wit: We have these really darling kids upstairs—three Boys. (Don't ask me what the "arrangements" are!) One of them, the blond, with hair down to here and eyes that see other worlds, is sweet on me. Strictly Oedipus-type thing, I mean it's not *voulez-vous coucher*, he wants to be in my *lap!*

Which I, Gloria of the barren marriage, see no harm in.

Tom, Tom, Tom, I'm not blaming *anybody* for the barren marriage, Ceil and Harry know we've chosen it thus, they know you're just bursting with seed. Pretty please, I'm trying to tell something, Tom, is nothing sacred?

Anyway!

I'm sitting here, gagging with boredom, at ten-thirty Friday night: Tom asleep in that chair, much as you see him now, mouth slightly open. *Very* attractive. Oh, Gloria wasn't bored. She was embalmed!

111

When *rap-rap-rap* on her chamber door, it's the blond one, Could he have some ice cubes, please. Looking like an archangel and his name is Michael! Can you bear it?

Nor can I.

So, just on an impulse, No, I said, I won't let you have a single cube, but you may have a drink.

Oh but, said he, finger pointing toward Heaven, I have these friends up there.

Ah well, the more angels the better, Go fetch them, I said. And while he was upstairs fetching I telephoned the liquor store.

Oh. Oh thank you, Tom, for that wonderfully salty contribution to my tale. Ceil and Harry are so grateful to hear all about the liquor bill. Now back to sleep, don't exhaust yourself, and we'll just see if I can't somehow manage to limp through without all this detailed assistance.

So.

I no more than hang up the phone when the parade begins. This lovely airborne parade. Angels and archangels. Cherubim and seraphim. All manner of winged creature, lighting gracefully on the furniture.

Slight hyperbole here: there were only three actually. Three Boys.

And this curious girl.

A dreadful little stump of a thing named Jo-Anne. All hair and horn rims. Truly. All you could see was its smock, its little fists, with ud-cray galore under its fingernails, *ça va sans dire*, and the most formidable hair. Virtually you could not see its face without trespassing. I haven't to this day the faintest notion of what the child looked like.

And yet, in retrospect, she managed, without speaking so much as a word that anyone heard, mind you, she saw to it that she became the star of the evening. Truly! This un-appetizing little bitch!

Wait! Wait! I have to tell things in my own way.

All right: I knew she'd been living up there with The Three, because I'd been seeing her for a couple of weeks, darting about the halls with pathetic little grocery bags. Making Herself Useful, I suppose. It seems Michael the Archangel had found her in the street in front of the Dom one morning at dawn, just sitting there inside of all this hair, and brought her home to make a little sister of her. Apparently they adore having little sisters.

(And mothers, a-ha-ha.)

So at one point, on ze glorious Friday night, Michael follows me to what we laughingly call the bar, that sad little tea wagon there, and wants to know what I think of his Jo-Anne. And I said, Michael, I haven't even seen her yet, what is all that hair about?

He looked at me with these ghost-blue eyes (Ceil, you'd faint!), and he said, perfectly serious, Jo-Anne's in hiding. From herself.

Oh, you idiot, Harry, of course I didn't laugh. What *am* I? Granted, inside, in here where it counts, I was split-ting. But not a flicker did I show.

Then Michael said, Gloria, I hope you'll try to bring her out, will ya? Try to get to know her a little? She's very worthwhile, she has all kinds of original thoughts, insights, ideas, she has her own little window on the world.

(Window! I thought; what the poor thing needs is a periscope!)

In any case, I was distinctly uneager, shall we say, to enter that red, unwashed wigwam. Treasure trove or no.

But anyway there we all were, having our otherwise

memorable and splendid Friday night: one of the Boys was doing perfectly thrilling things with his hands, an entire puppet show without puppets, *unbelievably* touching. And it was all wonderfully gay.

But a little too much so for Tom. Gay he doesn't mind if it's mixed, *un peu*. So I get on the blower once more and call Tom *deuxième*, who stage-manages at this coffeehouse over here, you know the one, Café Something, off-off-off-*off*-Broadway?

Seconds later in traipses he with the entire cast of this terribly integrated revue. And then Tom, my Tom, Tom *première*, really perks up. Tom likes Africans. Oh, he does he does he does! When I'm suntanned he can't keep his hands to himself. The dark shadow of Mama or something!

Oh look! Look! That brought him to life again! The sound of his own libido always does it. I have the most self-referencing husband in the world, I wish there were a contest I could enter him in.

Back to sleep, tiger.

Well now, with all this utter variety going on all over the place, I think—selfless being that I am—of all my dear square friends uptown. And I want them with me. I want them to see that Life Can Be Beautiful. So, on the blower again, dialing my fingies right down to the knuckles. *Come at once!* I shout to all and sundry; laughs, etc., at Gloria's. And Tom's.

I did call you!

Tom, how many times in all did I call Ceil and Harry? Eight, or was it only twenty?

Well, if people are mad enough to entomb themselves at the cinema on the first really brilliant night of the summer . . .

It was glorious. It was balmy. It was heaven replete with angels. All you could smell was life—and perhaps a little pot, ha-ha. We threw open that door to the fire escape, every window in the place, even the skylight, and let everyone flow at will.

Talk about heterogeneous! We had everything. Plus these performers. Oh, I grant you the revue itself stunk! (But isn't that always the way? By the time anything gets on the boards in this town, it's packaged to extinction.) But the kids! Themselves! The talent could kill you! I won't tell you about this one singer, not yet, I'm *saving* that! You'll die.

Where am I, for godsake?

Oh yes, the gnome. Jo-Anne.

At odd intervals throughout the evening or shall I say night, out of the corner of my eye, I catch its little act.

Nothing.

In short, it sits. A perfect lump. Inside of itself. Occasionally Michael goes over to it, puts his angel nose inside this disastrous hair and whispers to it. It whispers back. He puts his arm around it. He takes it to the roof for a breath of air. He guides it across the room to meet someone. He gives it a Coca-Cola.

(*Nota bene:* It doesn't drink hard liquor. Oh, no, not at all, my dears! Nothing so simple! *Wait* till you hear what's coming up!)

Now let's do a little montage of time pressing on: Me, this very matron you see before you, doing a watusi with the puppeteer (and quite good actually); Michael, trying to get his little catatonic to dance; Tom here, trying to get a little something *else* going on the roof.

He didn't hear that, just as well, I'd better whisper:

Yes, my Tom, Tom *première, not* cohabiting with Africans on the fire escape, and *not* very pleased about it. No thank you, said Miss Ghana. A stunning thing she was, too, *imperial,* and quite an artist of the put-down apparently. Tom doesn't know I had a full report.

What, Tom? Nothing, baby, you're just sensitive. Now nod off for Mama; that's it.

Isn't he heaven?

So! Emergency time! Michael, the guardian angel of the gnome, backs Mama into the bedroom! Yes, *me!* Too good to be true, surely!

Alas it *was* too good to be true: he didn't want Gloria, he wanted money.

Thirty-five smackeroos. Which is not thirty-five cents, need I add.

Good heavens, Michael, replied I, that's a great deal of money.

Oh, but he simply *had* to have it!

Frankly, he didn't look like he was kidding either, he was white as a sheet.

I said, Michael, are you in some kind of trouble?

No, but a friend of mine is, he said.

(Big light flashes on.)

Jo-Anne? I said.

Yes, she's sick, she's very sick. She's got to have some (and there was ever-so-tiny a pause) some attention! he said. She's got to have some *attention!*

(*Kleig* lights flash on.)

Drugs? I said.

Michael nodded.

H? I said.

H, he said.

And you want *me* to put up the thirty-five dollars to get her through this one?

You've got to, he said.

I've got to? I thought. My back went up. I adore this boy, but I don't *got to* anything of the kind. My poor Tom here works like a Trojan for thirty-five dollars, I felt guilty enough pouring out his good liquor for these young snot-noses. Which they swill happily, all the while I'm sure silently putting down Tom for being such a square as to actually practice anything so dreary as the law so he can come *up* with the money to finance a party. For them.

Frankly, it made me cross.

But Gloria did not blow her cool. All she said was, Michael darling, why have I got to? *I* can't afford such expensive vices myself, why must I support Jo-Anne's?

Because she's beautiful, he said. Because she's a human being. Because she's dying.

Dear Michael, I said, get her to a doctor at once if she's dying, don't come to me!

He said, Doctors file reports and Jo-Anne's too young to have her life ruined.

Well, yes, I said, there is a question of legality, isn't there. And you're asking me to involve myself? Please, I urged him, get the girl to a doctor!

(To be perfectly honest, I wanted her out of my house.)

He said he bet I wasn't so worried about legality at income tax time, or when I wanted an abortion. (He had me there! But of course the two things are not comparable!)

In any case he was furious, he absolutely *turned* on me!

Screw doctors, he said, screw cops, screw legislators, screw society! All she needs right now is one human being.

With which he turned on his heel and left the room.

I, of course, was the enemy.

Well, I went into ze dainty powder room and did what I could with a little cold water applied to the face. I'm damned, I said, if my night's going to be wrecked by that hirsute little junkie! Oh, I felt sorry for her, God knows, but there was just one teensy little question: *Whose* problem was it? Mine?

The answer to that didn't seem *too* tricky to me, so I went in and poured myself a good stiff one.

As a matter of fact, I think I'll fill this thing up right now.

Oh, would you, Harry? Thank you. Right to the top, and not too much ice.

No no no, the Scotch, damn it!

I did not shout.

So! Another montage. *Le temps marche*, it's now Saturday A.M., party still in progress.

I only remember seeing Michael once more, he was passing through the dining room saying, Is there a human being in the house, is there a human being in the house— looking bitter and grave and fugitive from Heaven; and that's the last I saw of him. Until . . .

Oh, but I know what's next: this song thing!

I won't be able to do justice to it, it's one of those things where you have to be there.

But I'll try:

At some juncture or other—I'm none too clear about time sequences—I came out of the bathroom and heard this fabulous silence. Everybody, all these young, wild things, standing stock-still, not uttering a sound. Well, well, wonders me, what's going on here?

Then I heard!

This singer was out on the fire escape. Singing to the rooftops.

You know that song from *Fantasticks:* try to remember a something September when nights are something and something is something else?

Well, this boy, an Italian, one of those three angels from above, with the most glorious tenor voice!

No! No, I'm wrong! *Not* really glorious! *Not* a great voice!

Merely perfect! Perfect for *that* song at *that* moment on *that* fire escape on *that* Friday night.

And everybody knew it. There was this enormous, collective sharing of something truly magical, and not a soul was excluded.

But that's not all. Something happened to top it.

You know where the end of the song goes: *Follow follow follow?*

Well! Just as he got to that part, there was a new voice! A woman's. We don't know where she was. We don't know who she was. We couldn't even see her. She was in some other building, way-way-way across the courtyards, leaning out of some dirty little window I suppose. And when our tenor was through, she picked it up in her sad little penny whistle of a voice; she sang: *Follow follow follow.*

I cried. Me, who doesn't cry any more. I cried. I'm crying now!

Everybody did. It was as if we were all seven, and pure again, and taking our first Holy Communion. Together. There was this feeling of the Oneness of humanity, the sort of thing Dostoevski raved about.

Excuse me, let me blow this nose.

Honestly, Ceil and Harry, I just adore this neighborhood. *So* it's noisy, *so* it's bearded and unwashed, *so* there are no taxis. You *take* all that, because it's alive!

Even if you are held responsible for murdering all the junkies. Don't you love that kind of thinking? It's terribly popular now. Some Negro playwright started it: the claim is that I, Gloria, personally adjusted the rope around every black neck that's been strung up in the U.S.A. for the last one hundred years. And of course it follows that this same dreadful Gloria is responsible for shelling out thirty-five smackeroos to save the life of every drug fiend in Manhattan!

Madly logical, don't you think?

Tom and I are strictly from Squaresville, we happen to think charity starts right here, we sort of look after each other first and foremost, don't we, sleeping beauty?

Never mind, dear, not important.

What?

The girl? Jo-Anne?

Well, I *said!*

Harry, I did!

Didn't I? Well, I know I did, I must have, that's what I've been going on and on about.

Forgive me, then, I *thought* I *said:* the poor little thing did indeed die.

Tom and I felt wretched, as you can imagine.

She died the next afternoon. I guess they were trying to do the withdrawal bit upstairs, you know, home style? And it just plain did not work.

I saw Michael in the hall that evening and he delivered the bare facts, looking—you guessed it, homesick for Paradise—and *so* tragic. And pointedly *not* saying I told you so.

I still adore him. It's just that once in a while he makes me a teensy bit cross.

THE
FRIGHT
OF
MRS.
YEAGER

Certain of Loretta Yeager's relatives up in Columbus, Ohio, had begun to believe it was high time she sold that damned trailer, lock, stock and barrel, packed up her few personal things, and got back home where she belonged. Her letters weren't just right any more, they said. Something was going on down there.

Several months earlier, in the parking lot of a West Palm Beach supermarket, Loretta, with no warning whatsoever, had become a widow. Inside the market, Ed Yeager, complaining of a dizzy spell after an altercation at the check-out counter—something about the price of tuna fish —had told his wife he'd wait for her in the Ford. But by the time Loretta had collected her change and green stamps from the cashier and started toward the door, a crowd had already gathered in the parking lot around her husband's body.

It happened that fast. Within a matter of seconds, Loretta had been forced to turn her mind from the planning of a veal casserole to that of a funeral for the person with whom she'd shared her life for the past fifteen years.

Then, on the very day of his funeral in Columbus, Loretta, against all the advice of her family, had reserved space for the return flight to Florida. The relative most opposed to this early return had been Loretta's older sister,

Ida, herself a widow for more than twelve years. She knew there was "something unwholesome" about it and began almost immediately in letters that varied in tone from a kind of affectionate wheedling to that of a downright, outspoken demand, to urge her sister's return.

Loretta was at first undisturbed by these letters. It was the prerogative of older sisters to give advice and make demands but they need not be listened to with more than one ear. Besides, Ida had been opposed to every major decision of her life; so it seemed to Loretta. At the time of Ed's retirement, when the Yeagers had first purchased their trailer, Ida had taken her aside to caution her:

"Oh, honey, I know it's romantic, even with a husband eleven years older than you, to just go where the wind blows. But listen to me: Ed's whole family has got a history of Sudden Heart in their fifties. I'm not being the least bit morbid either, you just name one Yeager man who's gone past fifty-seven. And where will it leave my Retta, all alone and God knows where. *Somebody's* got to be practical."

Eighteen months later, at Ed's funeral, Ida was able to restrain her tongue, but her eyes spoke out loud and clear, and, it seemed to Loretta, relentlessly for the whole three days: *I'm awful sorry, Retta, but what did you expect?*

The fact that she'd been *right,* and more than that, that she'd managed to refrain from saying so, seemed to have emboldened Ida to speak even more clearly on the subject of Loretta's new situation.

"A widow falls prey to all kinds of things," she warned at the airport.

And: "You'll go crazy down there!" were almost her last words as they embraced at flight time.

The first weeks of her grief passed slowly, but that was

to be expected. And of course she was lonely. Often she would awaken in the night and turn on the radio and cry and listen to the blues and think about her own solitude; and awaken in the morning with the radio still playing.

And later, when the weeks had become months, she would still catch herself speaking out loud inside the trailer as if she were not its sole inhabitant. "Ed, listen! Do you suppose we ought to . . ." But that was as far as she ever got before the emptiness of the place brought her up short.

Widowhood of course was new in the experience of Loretta Yeager, but it seemed to her there was some curious lack of focus in the character of her grief. Her thoughts were seldom of Ed but of Ed's absence. Actually she couldn't even conjure up any clear image of him in her mind. It was as if the man who died had not been a person at all, but a faceless occupier of spaces. That portion of the bed formerly occupied by him now caused in Loretta a kind of sickening terror that made her nights pure hell. In the mornings, try as she would to remember them, the specific events of her dreams eluded her completely. She knew only that her sleep had not refreshed her, and that in some unremembered darkness she had been the object of a terrifying and relentless pursuit. The only sleep that did her any good these days seemed to be in her brief catnaps at the beach.

She grew to abhor the emptiness of the bench across from her at meals. The sight of that yard of yellow plastic often produced in her a state of nausea so acute that at times she was unable to swallow her food. On certain mornings, following nights that were particularly disturbing, she would carry her breakfast outdoors and eat it there, seated on the trailer steps. Soon she found herself taking all three daily meals outdoors.

There was, then, in the mourning of Loretta Yeager, fear where there should have been sorrow. That was the long and the short of it. But she knew nothing of the ways of grief and perhaps her situation was normal. "The whole thing hasn't quite hit me yet," she wrote Ida in Columbus, "but I'm doing just fine and keeping busy and coming right along with it."

Ida after all was the last person in the world with whom she might discuss her true feelings. And who else was there? Loretta began to feel the need of someone to talk to. But she could think of no one at all. The friendships she and Ed had formed together seemed to be strictly husband-and-wife things. No one was ever alone. Everybody was part of a twosome. Besides, in the presence of these old acquaintances Loretta now felt—and she knew it was absurd, but there it *was*—that the five-foot-eleven, one-hundred-and-ninety-pound absence next to her was profoundly shameful. Sometimes on a chance encounter with someone who had known her and Ed together, she could hardly look the party in the eye.

It seemed to Loretta there was only one person in the entire state of Florida who would welcome a conversation with a lonesome widow. And when she thought of that one person, she shuddered.

This was Mrs. Kay.

Mrs. Kay was also a widow who did not seem to care much for the interior of her mobile home. She was the manager of the Southern Cross Trailer Court and maintained her office in a patio covered by an aluminum awning attached to the side of her neat twenty-footer. Mrs. Kay had arranged to do almost all of her living out of doors. She'd had a well dug in her garden and a hot plate installed, so that she not only ate there but cooked as well.

She was a colorful woman of sixty-plus who had about her such a perfect harridan air that it seemed to have been achieved through deliberate cultivation: she was over-dressed, overpainted, overperfumed, she talked too much and too loudly and what's more she seemed to know it and to enjoy your irritation with her.

There were always just enough extra bracelets on Mrs. Kay's wrists to make her seem awkward with the trowel as she puttered in her garden between cups of long-steeped jasmine tea, tea of which her guests could seldom endure more than a sip. And though she was usually as insensitive to their ears as to their palates, the lady did know how to talk interestingly enough. Ed Yeager in his day had seldom managed to pass the front gate without being drawn into conversation. Whenever he was late for a meal, or gone too long on a trip to the store, Loretta knew where to find him. "She can't shut up," he explained, "but there's something about the poor old broad. I like her."

Loretta did not. "I just don't think she's our kind of people" was the phrase she invoked to write the woman off; and since she was unaccustomed to probing too deeply into the reasons underlying her preferences and dislikes, the matter rested there.

Until Ed died. After that, she avoided Mrs. Kay as if the woman were an avowed enemy. Why? She didn't know, but she found reasons that served—for a while. The reasons were fairly thin: upon Loretta's return from the funeral, for instance, the woman had not offered one word of condolence. That alone seemed enough. "The way she acts"— Loretta thought about it a good deal these days—"you'd think I went up to Columbus on some fantastic *vacation*. Where does she think Ed *is* anyway?"

For Mrs. Kay, with no perceivable change of behavior

toward her, had continued to toss a smile and a wink and a Hello Honey at Loretta every time she passed the front gate, persisted in offering cups of that awful bitter tea that she knew would be declined; and she continued happily to accept, in exchange for these gestures, Loretta's icy nod of the head—as if that were precisely the response she had sought.

One thing more about Mrs. Kay—and this, to Loretta Yeager's thinking, was a little more complicated to think about but nonetheless potent in causing her to steer clear of the woman: she was depressing. Her eyes were sad. And her voice, even as she chit-chatted her way wittily and ruthlessly through the affairs of others, caught now and then on a certain unmistakably tragic note, telling of some dreadful private agony of her own that was never mentioned at all. Get close to a woman like that—Loretta believed without knowing why—and a person might even get *caught up* some way.

And so there was really no one to talk to, no one at all. And even while her solitude was causing distress so acute it sometimes amounted to actual terror, Loretta Yeager was unable to consider taking any real steps to alleviate it. She became so adept in eluding people that soon no one made any effort to talk to her at all. If a stranger at a lunch counter or somewhere tried to strike up a conversation, Loretta found she had lost faith in her powers of speech and had developed a kind of stammer that intensified her general state of fretfulness.

Ida meanwhile had not lost the scent of trouble. A long letter written at the end of June ended with the following post-scripted suggestion: "Loretta, honey, do you suppose one of these hot and sweltering miserable Florida summer days you'll be in the mood to put that trailer up for sale and come on home to your big sis?"

"Oh golly-ned, Ida," Loretta responded in her next note, "I just couldn't even think of selling this little gypsy wagon. Have made new curtains for it throughout and am waiting for a hobnail bedspread in two shades of green, no froufrou but very simple, to arrive any day now which I ordered from Spiegel's and am dying to see . . ."

Ida was alarmed and said so in a telegram:

PLEASE CALL ME REVERSE CHARGES IF YOU WISH BUT
MUST TALK TO YOU AS AM WORRIED SICK

LOVE IDA

This message reached Loretta as she was preparing her supper one Monday evening in July. She turned off the burners of her tiny stove and hurried to the office of the trailer court where the public telephone was located. Throughout the conversation she was aware of Mrs. Kay's ear somewhere in the vicinity.

She heard Ida's *Hello,* and *Oh yes of course she would accept the charges.*

And then: "Retta?"

"Ida?"

"Oh, Retta! You got my wire?"

"Yes, good lord, are you all right?"

"*I* am," said Ida. "I'm *fine*. But I just had to talk to my baby sister. Honey, we just don't know what's going on down there, and we're fit to be tied."

"Who is? What do you mean, Ida?"

"I mean, you doing that trailer over in new curtains, I couldn't understand a word of that. I called Ed's sister and we talked it over. . . Are you *there?*"

"Yes, I'm here," Loretta answered, "but I don't know what you . . ."

"So I called Elizabeth and read it to her and I said, 'Elizabeth, I can't make hide nor hair of it, can you?' And she said, 'Well, of course *I* know what Loretta's doing, she's just sprucing the place up so she can get a better *price.*' Elizabeth said she thought that was very smart. Sometimes a prospective buyer just falls head over heels for a bedspread or a cute lamp or something, and they want to move right in. Is that it? Are you there?"

Loretta said, "Oh, I just love you, being worried about me, Ida. I could almost . . ."

"Well, why shouldn't I be, all on your own down there. But is that it? What Elizabeth said?"

"You mean . . ."

"About upping the price with bedspreads, *you* know. Because what's it been now, honey, let's be realistic, Ed died in March, that's March April May June and my God in Heaven, this is July, do you see what I mean? Aren't you sweltering?"

"Me? Oh golly-ned, I've got the cutest fan! And we get a constant breeze anyway, just five blocks from the ocean here."

"March April May June and this is July, can it be five?"

"What?" said Loretta, "Months since Ed . . ."

"Just count it out," Ida said.

Loretta began to count. "March twelve to April twelve is *one;* April twelve to May . . ."

"You should have heard Ed's sister when I told her you hadn't even thought of putting it on the market."

"What's the date now, Ida? I know it's July because of the Fourth, but is it . . ."

"It's the seventeenth, I *think*. But did you hear me about Elizabeth?"

"Well then, we've *had* the Fourth, haven't we?" Loretta said.

"*Her* theory," said Ida, "is that you'd be a fool to think of selling it without putting it in A-1 shape."

"Ida, listen, I'd say it was just barely four months. Not that that's so all-important, but you know, it's not like *five* or anything. Now darn it all, you've got to stop worrying and don't let Elizabeth get you all whipped up. I could just kill her."

"It's not her! Loretta baby, it's *me!*" There was a long pause. When Ida spoke next, her voice had become calm: "Honey?"

"Yes. I'm here."

"You *are* coming back, aren't you, in your own good time? Without anybody rushing you?"

"Ida?"

"Aaawww. Is my baby crying? Is it lonesome? Does it want to come back to C'umbus where it's loved?"

"Oh Ida, I just can't stand to cry like this right on the phone."

"Tell me all about it, that's what I'm here for!" Ida said.

"Oh, I better just put it all in a letter. I've got to collect my thoughts and then I'll put it all in a letter."

"Put *what* all in a letter? What is it, what is it?" Ida was alarmed.

"Please, Ida, you've got to understand me, it's just I've got to collect my thoughts is all it is." There was a slight edge on Loretta's voice, every bit as hurtful to herself as it might have been to Ida. After a moment in which neither of them spoke, she said, "Ida? Please, Ida."

And then Ida said, "All rightee, precious, you put it all in a letter, but I want you to know I love you to pieces."

"Me too you."

"That's all I wanted to say, don't you see?"

There followed several more affectionate exchanges between the sisters. But for her part, Loretta's words were empty. She felt nothing. And the emptiness of her own heart made her fretful and ashamed.

When she had replaced the receiver on its hook, she looked at the telephone as if the failure of communication had been the fault of the instrument itself. "I can't help it," she rebuked it, "I've got to collect my thoughts."

This statement seemed to formalize a condition that had existed for some time, but which Loretta had been aware of only vaguely: in the weeks alone, her mind had gradually fallen into a state of disorder. It was as if its doors had been flung wide, a perpetual open house had been declared, and she had become the involuntary hostess to a thousand stray thoughts that flitted in and out on whims of their own over which she had little or no control.

For instance, in the past weeks, Loretta had been surprised by a series of events she had permitted to take place in her life, events in which she had been the prime actress but which seemed to have been the design of some stranger.

She had: emerged one day from a Lantana beauty shop with her hair color changed from what other women always referred to as "mousy brown" to a soft yellow that glowed like buttercups in the moonlight;

Not only changed the covers on her furniture but painted the inner walls of the trailer as well, and replaced all of the perfectly good dishes and many of the implements and fixtures in the place;

Purchased an entirely new wardrobe and sent the old one, every stitch of it, along with the old dishes, to the Miami headquarters of the Salvation Army.

For some reason unknown even to herself, she could give no serious thought to leaving either the trailer or the palm-shaded plot of land on which it was berthed. She seemed instead, with what amounted to an almost vigorous blindness as to purpose, to have set about camouflaging not only the place of her loss but the person who had sustained it as well. So thoroughly had she achieved this hiding of her former person that once, opening a letter from Ida, she felt she was reading somebody else's mail.

After the telephone conversation with Ida, Loretta sat on the edge of the bed looking at herself in the mirror. It alarmed her to realize she was in charge of the creature she saw there, this lusterless, talentless woman at the ragged end of youth with her grave, empty eyes and no gifts whatever for traversing the deserts of solitude that seemed to lie before her. "I can manage *two*," she said to herself aloud, "but I don't know what to do with one."

There. Perhaps she had begun to collect her thoughts. Once started, she resolved to continue. She spent the next hour seated at her kitchen table writing a time schedule of daily activities with which to discipline herself; and at the bottom of the page she wrote several resolutions of a more general nature:

See more people.
Be less alone with yourself.
Chat with other nice ladies.
Be on the lookout for someone to tell bad dreams to.

A few minutes later, Loretta, in her nightgown, was propped up in bed with a pad of stationery on her lap, half listening to the soft music from her radio.

"Dearest Ida," she wrote; and then, for the first time in months, she felt something that she told herself was happiness. But in reality it was only a moment of comfort. She was enjoying keenly a sense of safety in her own private room, the soft new colors of the place, the luxuries of having a plan for tomorrow and someone to write to.

Then, returning to her letter, all those pleasures suddenly lost their sweetness.

Ida had said, "Honey, you write me all about it." All about what? Loretta wanted to keep her promise, but she didn't know how. "Maybe I ought to tell her I've had my hair dyed. What if she does bawl me out, I'm forty-three, after all." But that wasn't it. She knew Ida didn't really care about hairdos any more than she had cared about the new curtains.

The longer she looked at the words *Dearest Ida,* and at the blankness of a page she couldn't fill, the sadder she became. Soon her room was no longer safe and private, it was merely empty, and even the newly arrived bedspread had lost its value for her. Now it only reminded her of the frenzy with which she had written the check to enclose with her order. "Doing the place over" had seemed such an exciting pleasure, with such a woman's-magazine wholesomeness about it; but now her sadness told her it was only the hysteria of someone whose life had been suddenly derailed.

"Oh, Ida," she said aloud, "if only I knew what to tell you!" She closed her eyes and wept softly to herself as the radio played some old wartime love song.

Loretta was awakened by a loud gasp that had issued from her own throat. She sat bolt upright in her bed like a person who has experienced some fright in her sleep. But she couldn't remember having slept at all. The lamp was on as before, the radio continued to play. Her bedside clock indicated that an hour had passed since she'd climbed into bed, but in her mind she could account only for a few minutes of it.

She began to look about for clues: a cigarette had burned itself out on the ashtray next to her bed. The stationery pad had fallen to the floor. She leaned over to pick it up and found that, in her own handwriting, these words had been written:

Dearest Ida,
He knows I'm still here.

In the morning, with a keen sense of the inevitability of her act, Loretta found herself settling into one of the plastic chairs in Mrs. Kay's aluminum-covered patio. She was given, to her surprise, not a cup of that dreadful tea but a perfectly brewed serving of coffee.

The woman, perhaps owing to the earliness of the hour —it was not yet nine o'clock—was as yet unpainted and unbraceleted. And what was even more surprising than her lack of adornment, Mrs. Kay seemed, for all her indiscriminating appetite for company, to be slightly weary of the visit even before it had begun. But the habit of hospitality was strong in her and she went through all the motions of being "positively delighted." All the motions but one: she did not look her caller in the eye.

There were a few awkward moments at the outset of

the visit, but soon Loretta found herself chatting as comfortably as she had once done with Ida.

"I'm having an awful lot of fun just talking like this," she admitted to Mrs. Kay. "For a while there I just couldn't seem to open my mouth. Can that be at all comprehensible to an outsider, I wonder?"

"Oh heavens yes," said Mrs. Kay. "Perfectly. Only what was it that finally broke it for you, that silent spell?"

"Well it was just plain getting unwholesome," Loretta said. "Your mind begins to play little bitty tricks on you, and pretty soon you just say to yourself, Look here, girl, let's pull ourselves together, huh?"

"I know," probed Mrs. Kay, "but what brought it about in particular?"

"You mean the particular thing that brought it about?"

"That's right, that made you want to . . ."

"Talk to someone?"

"Exactly."

"Well, in particular, let's see." Something within Loretta seemed to urge her to change the subject. But she found herself acting under some stronger more mysterious compulsion to withdraw the letter from the pocket of her slacks. "It was this."

She unfolded the piece of paper and spread it on the table before her. Mrs. Kay reached for it, but Loretta placed both hands on top of the letter.

"Just a second!" she said. "I have to give you the *preamble.*" She told Mrs. Kay some of the events of the previous night. "And this is what I found," she concluded, pushing the sheet of paper across the table.

When Mrs. Kay had read the words on the page, she continued to look at them for a long time. It seemed to

Loretta the woman was embarrassed by what she had read and didn't know what else to do with her eyes.

After a moment, Mrs. Kay mumbled *Oh dear* in a tone that seemed to carry no specific meaning—only a kind of weariness. She reached for the coffeepot and filled their cups, and then she slumped deep into her chair and looked at her own feet.

"I just didn't know who else to tell about it," Loretta said. She tried to laugh, but the effort failed. "Isn't it funny, the things that can happen? It certainly is lucky a person doesn't take every little thing too seriously. Now, don't you think so?"

"Oh yes," Mrs. Kay agreed but without enthusiasm. "A person doesn't dare."

"Did things like this ever happen to you?" Loretta asked. "I mean after . . ."

"Did I write letters in my sleep? No. But things just as foolish. I used to get people to stay with me. I was afraid to be alone."

"Well, that doesn't sound foolish at all! Didn't it work out?"

Mrs. Kay shook her head. "I ran out of people. They didn't need me. I needed them. And one by one they got fed up with me. It took me years to figure out why."

"I just don't understand that," Loretta said; and then she began to add a small lie. "You seem to be a very nice sort of person that . . ."

"Quit it, honey." Mrs. Kay stopped her. "You know as well as I do that I'm a thoroughly objectionable old lady." She gave a little token smile and shrugged her shoulders. "When you get to be my age and all you have to look back on is sixty-four years of selfishness, it's a little, um, *incon-*

venient to reverse gears all of a sudden." She glanced at Loretta, then looked away quickly. "Can you believe . . . Give me one of your cigarettes, will you?"

Loretta gave the woman a cigarette and a light. Mrs. Kay sat forward in her chair and continued. "Would you believe me if I said I had a man crazy about me for forty-one years, do you know how long that is, forty-one years?" She let out a cloud of smoke. Her mouth hung slack, giving her face a masklike emptiness. She stared straight ahead.

"Well, knowing *that*," Loretta said, "I should think you'd be very *happy!*"

"Oh, yeah?" said Mrs. Kay. "Well, here's the capper." She rested her chin on her hands, the cigarette trembled between her fingers. She swung her big eyes away from the gardenia plant on which they'd been held almost hypnotically and fixed them squarely on Loretta's. "I felt nothing for him. What do you think of that, nothing. But contempt."

Loretta tried to look away but her eyes were held vise-like by Mrs. Kay's. Something in the nakedness of the landlady's face gave Loretta a chill, and all of her old distaste for the woman returned with even greater intensity.

"I'm so sorry," she said, reaching for one of the empty phrases that had always sustained her in these social emergencies in the past. "I just, I just don't know what to . . ." Loretta was plainly flustered. She reached for her coffee cup, the stuff was too hot to drink so she put out her cigarette instead. "It's just such a—a *sad*—it's the *saddest* thing!" The landlady continued to look at her and that didn't help at all. Loretta wished people wouldn't tell such *personal* things, but she said, "I wish there was something I could say to—comfort you."

She rose from the table. "I've got a thousand things to

do," she said. "I haven't even had my bath, isn't that awful? Ooh!" she said, retrieving her letter from the table. "I'd better have *this!*" Then she laughed and said, "But what for, isn't that silly?" and crumpled it in her hand.

Mrs. Kay was still looking at her, her face was soft and her eyes were glowing. Loretta didn't know what was in that face now but she found it repulsive. And the staring was impertinent. No, it was downright rude. It was time to have it out. Loretta stood still and returned the stare.

"Why are you looking at me like that?" she demanded, hoping the woman couldn't hear the hysteria in her voice.

"No reason, dear." Mrs. Kay looked away. "Well, better get on with our days, hadn't we." She began to clear the cups from the table.

Loretta said nothing.

When she had walked several yards down the lane, she turned to glance over her shoulder and found Mrs. Kay standing in the middle of her patio still looking at her with the same naked, depressing stare.

Under her breath, Loretta said, *"Die. Disappear. Turn to ashes."*

But when Mrs. Kay waved at her, she waved right back.

TERRIBLE
JIM FITCH

A one-act play

(*Playing time: one hour*)

THE SETTING: *An inexpensive motel room located on a highway near Albuquerque, New Mexico. It is daytime but the window shades are drawn so that it appears to be night. The most prominent piece of furniture in the room is an iron bedstead, but there are also a vanity table and bench, a chest of drawers and some chairs. The arrangement of personal belongings might indicate that the inhabitants are used to making themselves at home in temporary places. On the floor near the bed is a small wooden ukulele painted blue.*

THE ACTION: SALLY WILKINS *comes in, leaving the door wide-open. She wears a slouch hat, a trench coat and high-heeled shoes. Her face is partly hidden by the brim of her hat and by the turned-up collar of her coat. It is clear from her general attitude that* SALLY *is in a depressed state. She goes to the vanity table and sits motionless in front of the mirror. After a moment she reaches into a drawer and withdraws a jar of cold cream, removes the lid and begins*

145

*to smear the mirror with white. But this project cannot
hold her interest for long. She leaves it undone, slowly
wiping her fingers with tissues. After another motionless
moment, the bed begins to claim her attention. She seems
to lean toward it, drawn by it.*

*A man appears in the open doorway, carrying a six-
pack of beer. Unnoticed by the woman, he watches her
movements. This man is* JIM FITCH. *He wears vaguely
Western clothing, appears to be a kind of cowboy—but as
the play unfolds there arises some question as to where he
would be most at home, in the saddle or on Times Square.
He has a wild aspect, this* JIM FITCH, *like a creature someone tried to tame by cruel methods that failed. He is sometimes a little punchy, but always on the alert for treachery
from others; at moments he is extravagantly joyful, as if
dazzled by the miracle of his own survival. His own ha-
bitual attitudes are at the moment suspended as he watches
the woman. Slowly she rises, and like one surrendering to
a power more considerable than her own will, she goes to
the bed and lies on it. Now* JIM FITCH *carries the un-
opened beers to the dressing table. When he has looked for
a moment at the mess of cold cream on the mirror, he
takes a drink from the can in his hand, and speaks.*

JIM FITCH

The manager of this motel just asked me if something
was wrong with my woman. I told him to shut his goddam mouth. Then I figured what the hell, so I grinned at
him—you know how I do, tee-hee?—and made out like I
was joking. And I said no, everything's fine, thank you, my
woman is a little down in the dumps here of late, but it'll
pass. Then he started in talking about a slew of women he

knew of. And they was all down in the dumps, all forty-four hundred of 'em.

I wanted to tell him to shut his goddam mouth all over again. But I just walked away.

Anybody want me to open 'em a can of beer?

Why, there's Lonesome Sally Wilkins, over on the bed! And what's this?

(*He picks up the ukulele.*)

Why, I believe it's—yes it is—it's her blue ukulele!

I wonder if she'll talk to me.

(*He goes to the bed, leaning on the iron bedstead, and looks down at her, speaking with great and real tenderness.*)

Lonesome Sally. I am returning to you your blue ukulele.

I love you, Lonesome Sally. Terrible Jim loves you to death. Yes he does. You want me open you a can of beer?

(*No answer from* SALLY. JIM *walks back to the dressing table.*)

I'm gonna open Sally a can of beer.

There! I have opened her a can of beer.

Hey, pretty thing. I'm holding a can of beer out to you here.

Well, I'll just set it here for you on the floor, for when you want it.

(*He places the beer on the floor next to the bed.*)

He asked me, the manager of this place, he asked me if you was some famous person. I suppose 'cause you're so pretty and your heels are so high and your hair's so lovely, you must've put him in mind of some famous person. I can't blame him thinking that. Shoot.

I said, well, technically no, my woman is not world-famous, but she knows how to walk into a saloon and put the jukebox out of business. And she was on the radio once in Brownsville, Texas. Sang one little song on her ukulele, and five minutes later the switchboard was jammed with people calling up, inquiring. And for years after, the post-cards was still rolling in, all of 'em wanting to know who was the owner of that lonesome, beautiful voice that sang "When My Blue Moon Turns to Gold Again." Well, I told him how I give that Brownsville radio station permission to announce that the singer in question was a lovely lady name of Lonesome Sally Wilkins. *But!* Sad as it may be for the public at large, Lonesome Sally was now the personal and private property of one Jimmy K. Fitch of Decatur. I—uh—went on to admit that this Jimmy K. Fitch was pretty much of a no-account, with a criminal mentality to boot, and clearly, he don't deserve to be the only person in the whole wide world nowadays that gets to listen to the voice of Lonesome Sally Wilkins singing songs on her blue ukulele.

But he is.

Yes, I told the manager of this motel—this person, this Terrible Jim, gets any song he wants any time he want it: "Oh Careless Love," "Too Late to Worry, Too Blue to Cry," "I Can't Stop Loving You," "When My Blue Moon . . ."

(*The woman turns over.*)

Did you think I was asking you to sing me a song now? I am merely repeating to you a conversation I had with the manager of this motel. And you, you thought I was asking you to, ha, to sing me a song?

Well, you're wrong. You just don't listen to a person. You sure don't. If I was in the mood to hear a song, you would know it, they wouldn't be any guesswork about the thing. I'd say, All right, Sally, I want "The Streets of

Laredo," and you'd take up that mother- . . . (*indicating the ukulele*) . . . and you would goddam well pick out "The Streets of Laredo" on it. And you would sing, lady, yes you would, no matter what mood you was in, hear me? You understand? Yeah, I think you do.

What I'd like to hear now, I'd like to hear the sound of that ukulele cracking over . . .

Agh, to hell with it.

(*At the window*) In case anybody thinks I am crazy about this weather—well, I'm not! I don't like it any better out there than I do in here. So what chance have I got.

(Jim *takes a swallow of beer, looks at the can with disgust.*)

Aaagh, I hate this stuff. I've lost m'taste for beer altogether. Drink it more to keep m'throat wet than anything else, purely a matter of maintaining some level of bodily humidity, but they's no pleasure in it.

(*He lights a cigarette.*)

Same with these damn things. I hate 'em with all my heart. Love lighting 'em up, striking the match, blowing out the flame, up to there I'm fine. But after one puff, the whole thing goes kerflooie on me.

That takes care of beer, cigarettes. What else is there, food? I am fed up with food, too. I am fed up with practically anything you can name. Fed up with the weather, fed up with this room, fed up with you, fed up with New Mexico and new this and new that—'cause it's all *old*.

I am fed up with breathing. Look at this! Take it in, let it out, take it in, let it out; Christ, I wish I could think up a substitute for breathing; I'd make a million dollars.

(Jim Fitch *settles into a chair.*)

Sally. I opened a can of beer for you. I set it there for you, on the floor.

Now, um, if you was to reach out with your, uh, left arm, keeping it horizontal and parallel to the bedstead, that is at a ninety-degree angle to your own body, then lower it, I'd say eleven inches, eleven and a half, and wiggle your middle pinky—well, I believe you'd get it wet. Go ahead. Then lick it off and see if that don't give you the taste.

Trying to make things easy for you today, little lady. Hence, the highly detailed, precision instructions on how to get at that beer with a minimum of effort.

Don't care for that plan? Well, now, let's give it some more thought then. Seems to me with my *criminal mentality* I ought to be able to come up with something here. How would it be if I was to come over and hand it to you? Or pour it down your gullet for you?

Don't care for that either, do you? You don't seem to have a whole lot to say here lately, do you, little Sal, my pretty gal? Is that some kind of a new wrinkle? I guess you're fed up, too, is that it? Fed up with conversation, fed up to the point where you don't even grunt any more?

That kind of worries me.

And tell the truth, I'm a little worried about that hat staying on, too, and that hair pulled over y'face like that. Now, when we come in the door here, I fully expected to see that hat come off, and the coat, too. I didn't even give the matter much thought. I just fully expected them garments'd be removed as a matter of course! But that is not what took place here; no, not atoll. What took place was you just kept yourself covered up. That surprised me. I'm gonna be honest about this thing; it hurt me. It hurt me! I suppose I have somehow always pictured myself as the kind of a simple-ass son-of-a-bitch a person could show his face to, isn't that a laugh?

You going to keep your collar up forever? And your hat pulled down forever? I am opposed on principle to anybody going around hiding his face, especially forever.

Sal, the thing you don't realize is, it just calls attention, more attention. Person'll think, what's the matter with that fine-looking woman, collar pulled up and hat yanked down that way? They don't know you're merely hiding a couple weensy little scars. No, Christ no, they put their minds to work on it, and they figure you must be hiding about four hundred big purple sores with green pus coming out of 'em. A person's mind has got this tendency to make things worse than what they are. You follow my point or not?

Take that waitress. Back at the drive-in? Her mind was on fire, couldn't you tell? She was itching to get a good squint at that face of yours. What you think she was hanging around for, making all that jackass conversation?

Now you might think she was on the make for me. Well, she was, that's only natural. But that was just the half of it. The other nine-tenths of her was praying to Jesus she'd catch you off guard and get one good healthy eyeful.

(*He walks over to the bed.*)

I'm going to set down here and I'm gonna tell you the truth: I believe you look better with them scars. Fellow look at you now, he'll think, Hey, that beautiful lady is nobody to fool with! Whereas, before, frankly, you could've been mistaken for some kind of a pushover. Pretty as hell, but possibly a pushover. Hear me? Sal?

Sally! Did you shiver? You shivered. Oh. Oh. Oh my God. That's the first time my Sally ever shivered from me just saying her name. And I said it nice. I know how I said it; I know all about saying a person's name, they's a thousand ways to do it. You can make it like *"Sally!"* Like a knife you're trying to cut 'em up with. But that's not how

I just done it. I went at it easy. Should've made you feel like I was rubbing your back: "Sally darling," I said.

Didn't I?

Hey, are you listening to me?

I said, are you hearing me?

Uh, listen here, Miss Lonesome, I am sorry you got your face messed up. I am damn sorry you got your face messed up. It's an awful goddam pity it had to happen. But mark you, baby, I am Jimmy K. Fitch and I am the same Jimmy K. Fitch I was last week; and Jimmy K. Fitch rhymes with son-of-a-bitch, and that means when I talk I like to see ears quiver.

(JIM *goes to the dressing table for a fresh beer.*)

Maybe you'd rather have a Coca-Cola, you want a Coca-Cola? There's a machine in the office.

Oh, I guess you think I'm a pretty terrible person. Terrible Jim, is that it? Mm-hmm, yeah, uh-huh, I know, all my life I been terrible. That's what they all called me in Decatur. Hit that town from Arkansas when I was thirteen; and right from the start, every mama in town would say to her kid each morning, "Don't let me catch you playing with that Terrible Jim Fitch." They all said that.

Every mama but my own. My own mama never called me nothing worse than darling. "Good morning, darlin' Jim, come here to me."

Hug.

"Hey, darlin' Jim, I brought you a present from Cincinnati; close your eyes." You see, my mama was a hooker just like you, but she knew how to say darlin' to a man and make it stick. Last time I heard that voice I was thirteen and it was on the telephone from St. Louie. She said, "I am comin' to fetch you in the morning, darlin' Jim. Bye."

So I got into my drawers and set up on the front porch all night. But . . .

It's just as well she never come for me, never found out what kind of reputation I was beginning to enjoy. Reputation, hell, it wasn't nothing short of fame. I was famous through there, Sal. Southern Illinois, all through there I was famous. I got a kick out of it, too. I enjoyed it.

'Cause, see, I got this *criminal mentality* where I enjoy being called a terrible person. You didn't know that? Oh, yeah, it's a fact. I was told that. By a woman't claimed she was crazy about me, too. A very, uh, religious woman, very intelligent, too, knows all about Jesus and psychology and Heaven.

(*He is referring to* SALLY.)

Well, it was her said I had this thing, *this criminal mentality*. Said my case was extremely extreme, which accounts for why I like to rob churches. Can you fancy that, Sally? Here I always thought I liked robbing churches 'cause they was easy. But it turns out that's got nothing to do with it. *Why?* she says, *why* is it robbing churches is so easy for you? Well, I said, because they's nobody tending 'em! No no no, she says, the *real* reason!

I wanted to puke.

Wonder how it is that somebody's supposed to be so crazy about you can just set around thinking up dirty words for you. Makes you feel lonesome.

But I got no cause to be lonesome, not any more. 'Cause nowadays and henceforward, they's two terrible people around here, one with this terrible mean streak in him, me, and one with the terrible fa- . . .

(*The withheld word is face.*)

I didn't mean that the way it sounded, kid, not by a long shot.

Sal, listen to me, you are one good-looking gal, always was, always will be. I am proud to be traveling around with such a good-looking gal. All I meant when I said terrible was . . .

Sal, I'm going to have to be truthful about this thing: you was getting *too* perfect there for a while, you was getting too pure. That's all right for a little virgin to go around looking like a bunch of buttercups, but when that little virgin gets to be a woman—and a hooker to boot; yeah, hooker—then something's got to take hold of that face and give it a little—a little something to show she knows how to take her lumps.

Ex-hooker?

Oh. No kind of hooker atoll any more, is that it? Not even ex?

Well! That's a crying shame, 'cause the lady I took a tumble for was a hooker lady. And a damn fine one. Are you not that lady? Did I not meet you in the passion pit at the Lavender Fawn in Key West, Florida? Or are you some other lady altogether? Let me see your face.

Oh, Lord, 'scuse me, I said "face" again, didn't I!

Shoot. This won't do atoll. We got to get you straightened out, Sal. We got to get you pulled together. We got to initiate some kind of rehabilitation program. We got to assist little Sal in getting accustomed to showing her face.

What we'll do, we'll go out and find us a crowd of people. Maybe drive in to Albuquerque. To the bus depot. They's always a crowd of people in the bus depot in Albuquerque. You ought to know, you used to work it.

(*For a moment, he seems to be overtaken by some vaguely disturbing memory.*)

Now, um, where was I in my thoughts here. I had

something I was driving at. The bus depot, the bus depot.

Oh! I know! Program; now listen: we go there. And that hat with the wide brim, you leave that in the damn Ford, *outside.*

(SALLY *instinctively raises her hand to her face.*)

And your hands, you'll put them in your pocket and leave 'em there. Then I'll just march you right into that bus depot, in the heart of downtown Albuquerque, with that fine face poking right out in front of you. And you'll stand there. And you'll let 'em look at you. Just like before.

Know what you'll find? You'll find 'em looking at your pretty eyes, and your pretty hair, and your pretty legs, just like they always did. I swear to it. I swear to you the women'll be wishing they was you; and the men'll be trying to puzzle out how they can get next to you, exactly like before. And I'll bet you my half interest in that Ford out there not one person will pay the least attention to them puny, pathetic, weensy little scars.

And if they do . . .

Listen, Sal, here's what. While you're standing there, in that bus depot, guess where I'll be. I'll be just kind of inconsequentially setting on a bench, not more'n twenty foot away, see? And not paying the slightest attention, hell no, not even looking—'cept out of the corner of my eye. And I don't have to tell you, do I, that I see more out of the corner of my eye than most folks see out of a frigging binocular?

So! I'll be setting on this bench. Waiting. The first mother's son that lowers his big-ass orbs for one split second on them scars of yours and wiggles so much as an eyebrow . . .

What can I say, Sal, what can I tell you? That person, that poor unfortunate and extremely unlucky mother is going to run straight into Mr. Ruthless Awful Terrible Old Me. Oh, I could cry, could cry right now, for that poor, poor person, whoever he be, be he white or black or pink, that looks at your scars for one split fraction of an infinitesimal scrap of a goddam unhappy second. Well, I tell you what I probably be forced to do.

I be forced to put him on the floor. Somehow. Neat. And then I'll lift up this big foot, and I'll take that poor mother by the face and . . .

(*The unspoken words: "and grind it into him!"*)

(JIM *is stricken with regret for a memory he has evoked. There is a long pause in which the mood changes entirely. He is utterly lost for a moment until he finds himself suddenly in anger.*)

Get up, Sal. I want you up off that bed. Now.

(*And then compassion.*)

Na, hell, you don't have to get up. Today.

Today I'm gonna let you lie there. Not gonna make you talk either. 'Less you want to of your own accord.

I want to do the right thing by you, Sally. 'Cause you just had one hell of a shock to your system. When a person gets messed up and then he takes the bandages off and gets a good squint at hisself in the mirror, well, it's some shock. To his system. So today, you just do as you please.

Me? Oh, poop, Sal, it don't matter what I do, I'm all right. (*At the window*) The sky has been going all day long from all blue to all black. One minute seems like it might be studying to rain, next minute the sun's up there going tee-hee tee-hee; shee-it. I'm staying put, staying right here with my gal.

I believe I'll play the radio.

No, I'm damned if I will. Twenty-five cents an hour, why that's just thievery. They get you in here on a rainy day, see, and they shove this coin box at you, paint it bright red, look, see that? Bright red. And they figure you'll either jam it full of quarters or go nuts! Well, to hell with them.

(*He kicks it.*)

Sal? Sally. I hope you didn't fall asleep on me.

(*He forces one of her eyes open with his thumb.*)

Hell, I knew you hadn't done that to me. 'Cause you know how I hate that, to talk and not be heard.

Listen, Sal, screw the radio. Any time I get in a pinch, or trapped somewhere, or waiting on the rain to quit, I make use of my time; I am a man with inner re-sources; I got m'philosophy to work on. Believe it be a good day for it, rainy.

All great men do that, you know: Beethoven, Einstein, what they do, they figure out a system. Now the general run of people think philosophy is something complicated, and deep. Nah, not atoll. Philosophy is nothing but a system of angles you figure out to keep from going nuts in some motel room. It's all in the world it is.

I ever tell you about my friend Silas in San Pedro? Silas was not a composer. Actually he was a pimp. And a fine man, never nervous about anything. Now Silas was a man with a system. Trouble was he was part Indian, and Indians don't talk much so I never did learn what his system was. I believe it had something to do with smoking marijuana.

That don't work for us though, does it, Sal? We just get hungry. Every time you and me light up, we start in eating like a couple horses and acting a fool.

(*He laughs, stopping abruptly.*)

Person's got to have some system. There was a while I thought I had me one. Come to me in a dream.

How it happened was, I got in a fistfight one night in Key West. Got *my* face all mashed up that night. And when I went to sleep . . . no, it wasn't night, it was daylight; and I was sleeping in the back seat of a car. I don't know whose car it was. Some stranger owned that car.

Now, um. Now, goddammit, I'm losing my point.

What am I talking about, Sal, something about sleeping in cars? Help me!

Answer me, goddam you. . . . Some day, some day, lady, you are not gonna answer me, and God help . . .

I got it! Sleeping in cars! One night in a saloon in Key West, I got in a fistfight and when it was daylight I went to sleep in a car and had this dream about philosophy. There! I remembered—without anybody helping me.

Now, the dream: I dreamt I was sleeping not in any back seat, but in a great big mother-grabbing room, and in this room was every son-of-a-bitch in the world. I mean every man woman and child black white and yellow, and every wild tiger and every little puppy dog and every goddam grasshopper. That room had everything that's alive in it.

And you know what we was doing? Me and all them Chinamen and old ladies and all them animals and kids and insecks, et cetera? We was in there praying together; eyes closed, setting still, and praying. Can you imagine that, Sal, me with my criminal mentality, having a dream about praying?

Well, here's the twist; we wasn't praying to God, no, not by a damn sight! We was praying *about* Him. We was praying He wouldn't get us. Yeah, you heard me. We was all in there, in this big room, and He was outside coming at us, God; and the way it was was: one at a time, He could take us—but if we stuck together, He couldn't. See?

So all us live creatures was banded together in that room, safe. It was the sweetest damn dream, Sally. It was like— uh, Sal, do you remember sucking on your mama's titty? I do. I remember drinking my mama's milk; and that's how the dream was. Safe and sweet. They wasn't anybody gonna grab your ass. Not even God. 'Cause like I said, if we stayed together, God was gonna quit bugging us. He was gonna cool it. He was gonna turn the misery valve down for a change; flip the lonesomeness switch off. No more bad news; no more bad dreams; no more sleeping alone; or with a cold woman. All that crap was gonna cease!

I woke up thinking I had me a system. And I was tickled pink, too. Face bleeding, nose busted, one eye swollen shut; but I had the world by the short hairs! 'Cause I knew this secret: get everybody to stick together and God will let up on you.

Well, let me tell you, that little notion about cost me my butt; they wasn't a one soul I told it to but thought I was trying to put something over on him; or else I was some kind of mental defective.

You see, if you got a system depends on everybody in the world agreeing with you—forget it. That system is no good, it is worth exactly zero. What you got to have is a kind of system that works when you're all alone.

And they's only one little bitty hitch; they's no such animal.

Listen to me, Sal. I'm experienced. I been on the road all my life, and I state flatly—when you're all alone, they isn't nothing works.

Oh, you poor thing, you think you got it so bad, don't you, traveling around with terrible me, just 'cause I'm a little mean once in a while; just 'cause I messed up your face a tiny bit.

Well, there's one thing even worse can happen to you: you just go on out on that road—alone. Go. Go ahead. I'll let you take the Ford, it's yours.

Here, I'll even pack your damn suitcase. Here's your panties, here's your bazeers, here's your cashmere sweaters. Your war paint, your cold cream, your eyelash curler. Here's your *eyelashes!*

And half the money. I'm putting it in your pocketbook. I believe you'll find a good hundred and fifty in this wad; that ought to be enough, Sister Sal, to get you to the nearest, uh, convent.

And here is one blue ukulele.

And the car keys. Yeah. I give you the Ford. And I give you the open road, and I say go. *Vaya con Dios* all by yourself alone and see how you like that awhile.

Well. Why don't you move? You got my word of honor I will not move a finger to stop you. I know you don't take much stock in the word of honor of a person with a criminal mentality, but here's a good time to try me.

(Sally Wilkins *sits up and looks at the suitcase with her pocketbook, the ukulele, and the car keys on top of it. After a moment, she allows herself to fall back on the pillow. Jim Fitch is clearly relieved. When he speaks, it is with complete sincerity.*)

I'm glad you decided to stay. 'Cause I'd miss you something awful.

But they isn't nothing going to change much, you know that, don't you? As long as you're with me, you'll be living on the net proceeds of my church work. I'm too old now to change my style, Sally. Some people part they hair on the right, some on the left. Well, I don't part my hair atoll. I rob churches. Oh, when I was younger I used to think about it plenty, other ways of making a living. And

I've tried 'em. I've hustled, I've pimped, I've pushed, I've conned, I've done stores and private residences, all them things. But I am a church man. Hardest thing in the world for me is pass up a church. I just got to try the door, and if it's unlocked—that poor-box is a goner.

Did I ever tell you about the time in San Antone I run into some nuns in my work? Well: one time in San Antone, I was working St. Something-or-other's. St. Cecilia's? I don't know. Anyway I heard this noise. Sound like it was coming from the basement of the church. So I thought I better investigate. And I went in the back and found the stairs and went on down. And there was these two little nuns setting at a big table. Must've been a Monday morning, 'cause they was opening collection envelopes. One of 'em was real pretty and she was busy with the scissors cutting off the ends of the envelopes and dumping the money out on the table. Folding money, too, most of it. And the other'n, the ugly one, was counting it up and writing in a book. Well, I couldn't believe my good fortune. I just stood there, astounded. Finally the nuns looked up, and we stared at each other for a while. Then this little cute one said, "What do you want?" And I said, "Well now, sister, since you ask, I believe I'd like to have some of that money." Then the other one spoke up, Sister Mary Ugly, and she said, "This money belongs to God." So I said, "Let me take it to Him, honey; I know a real good shortcut." And I walked over and I gathered up about three hundred dollars, couldn't have been easier, it was like picking dandelions. When I was leaving, the cute one said, "Aren't you ashamed of yourself; you look like such a nice man." "Oh, sister," I said, "I am a nice man. Why, I go to church ever' day of my life." Course, I don't suppose she caught the humor of that.

Neither do you, huh?

That's too bad. Cause what I'm doing, I'm trying to keep this motel room, these walls here, from putting the squeeze on the both of us. Figure as long as I keep talking, we won't neither one of us bust out of our heads. These motel rooms, Sally, they're dangerous, you stay in 'em too long.

Hey, let's go find us some space.

I never had a room yet was big enough. Sally, I think I be perfectly to home and cozy in a goddam cathedral! How come is it I always end up in some smelly little closet of a place like this?

I believe this room is gaining on me.

(*He cocks his head, as if listening for a voice in the silence.*)

Yeah. Yeah, it is. Oh lord. And I think my voice is about give out, too.

Baby, it is time for you to talk. Now I am a rational animal, and I am talking quiet and simple and logical: we got an emergency here. You pick some subject fast. Anything under the sun, cabbages and kings, or how it was when you was a little girl; or eeny-meeny-miney-moe; or about your daddy dying. Hey, you can tell me all about your daddy dying if you want to. But talk.

I need the sound of a voice.

Sally! Are your lips moving?

Are you trying to say . . .

No.

No, I don't believe it.

I can't believe it.

The woman is praying. The woman is actually talking —to God. I think I'll beat her up.

Why, they must be a million people all over the world

yapping at Him right this second, singing at Him, mutter-
ing at Him, ten thousand church organs pumping away,
forty thousand pianos and a million tambourines. Now
you'd think, wouldn't you, that he could leave me alone
with my one little woman and a seven-dollar ukulele
painted blue?

Nope. No, the Good Father wants it all.

Yeah! The Good Father.

Well, you go 'head and pray. While I tell you a few
things about that Big Buddy of yours: I believe His reputation is just ever-so-slightly out of whack with the facts. I'll
go farther. I'll say the only thing halfway to His credit is
Him making the world to be such a pretty place. But not
for you to look at, and not for me to look at. Nah, baby,
we're just people, and people are too scared and ornery
to see straight; it's for Him, for Hisself to look at—way
up there away from the stink and misery: floods, train
wrecks, wars, starvation, diseases, the heat and the cold
and the lonesomeness. Yeah, that's His style: set the place
on fire and scoot off to Heaven to enjoy the flames. You
honest and true think if I pull that kind of crap they going
to come around to me lighting candles and singing songs?
Yeah, I bet.

But He don't have to follow His own rules: nope. He
give your daddy cancer and what you do? Fell on your
knees and got religion, didn't you? And then I come along.
And for awhile I believe you like me even better'n you
liked Him. Maybe you thought I was meaner. I'm not. Oh,
I'm mean; but I can't hold a candle to that One.

Funny; I'll bet you're lying there right now thinking
about how sweet it's gonna be in Heaven—away from
Terrible Jim. What a laugh; sweet? With Him runnin' it—
that ukulele-grabber? Suppose, when you died, Sal, you

found out Heaven was just another Albuquerque. What would you do, would you vomit? Know what I'd do? If I died and found out Heaven was just another Albuquerque? I'd go to the bus depot and get me a ticket to Hell, express. Yeah, I think I get along better with the devil running things, thank you. He's probably just some poor old pimp—like my friend Silas in San Pedro. Him and me always got along okay. So I'll get on a bus to Hell. Which will probably be another San Pedro—or Times Square or Tia Juana or Dallas—and I'll make out all right. I can make out in places like Hell: I've had practice.

But not you, you're studying for something sweet and lovely, bands playing, angels on the march. Baby, I hope for your sake they's a real Heaven somewhere, and I hope it's halfway decent. Just look at you, all alone and miserable, praying for help from that deaf old thing up there.

If I was God, I'd hear you.

Know what I'd whisper to you? I'd say, "Hey, you down there, Sally Wilkins, all scrunched up hiding herself on that bed in the Wild West Motel, Route 66, U.S.A. This is God talking. I see you. I hear you praying. You lonesome thing. And I got a answer for you. Just lift up your hand, or one little pinky of it, and beckon to that big snake of a man there, that what's-his-name Jimmy K. Fitch that loves you so. And he'll rush right on over to you, and he'll lie down with you, and you just forget all about that criminal-mentality crap, and you let him give you something good.

"And after, you take up that little uke, pick out something blue on it, and let him listen to it with you. And that'll be what Heaven's like. Almost."

(*In his own voice*) Baby, if you want to, you can tell me how sore you are at me. You may have some grudge.

Who knows, you may still blame me for your face; you may not realize I am constitutionally unable to hear bad things about my mentality. Well, you just say so, it's open season, anything at all is hunky-dory—just so it's out loud where I can hear it.

You know, I am none too crazy about certain facets of my own personality. If I could, I'd get rid of 'em. If I could. Take this mean streak of mine. Now, if I knew where that was located in me—say it was a vital organ, a heart or a kidney or a lung, and I knew where it was—I'd take this knife, and I'd cut it right out of me. Yeah, mm-hm, I would. The blood would be squirting and it would hurt like holy hell; but I would keep on cutting till it was all gone, keep cutting it out of me till what was left was a—a nice person. I would do that.

And then you would set up and you would look at me. And you'd say, "Hi, Jim darlin,."

And I'd say, "Hey! Sally darlin'."

And you'd say, "Let's get out of this awful little room, let's go to Mexico."

And I'd say, "Wh-wha-what's that, kid? Mexico? You want me take you to Mexico?"

And you'd say, "Yeah, Jim, I sure would like that, darlin'."

And I'd say, "All right, hell, I can afford it. I got half the building fund for the First Methodist Church in Santa Fe right here in my pocket, I'll take you wherever you want to go. You want Mexico, let's go to Mexico. We'll just wind up the Ford and *phhhhht* right on down and get lost there, South of the Border. If I got sleepy at the wheel you sing that to me, will you? "Down Mexico Way—that's where I fell in love . . ."

I beg y'pardon? Oh, yes, yes of course.

(*He takes the ukulele and places it in her hand.*)

MM. That's nice.

(*He hums.*)

Lovely.

Just a tiny bit louder.

Sal.

Sally, honey.

(*Singing:*) I wonder what's become of . . .

(*An angry shout:*) SALLY!

(*She pushes the ukulele away from her and it falls to the floor.*)

Hey now, that got you, didn't it? Only thing is, it hurts my throat to holler, I'm so hoarse already.

So you talk up now. And you tell me what it is you're holding out for.

Just what is it you want?

Now you're gonna have to give me a clue.

Is it got something to do with this knife?

Lord, I suppose that manager out there was smarter'n he thought he was, asking me if something's wrong in here. I believe he was right. I believe they's gonna be some bad news come out of this room today, here in the Wild West Motel, big bad news.

The lady wants me to kill her.

And I'd do anything for this lady; wouldn't I?

But kill her? Lord, I don't believe I'm in the mood for that.

I wish I had a cat or a dog or something small to warm up with. Here! I believe this ukulele'll do. Let's see here now.

(*He smashes the ukulele against the bedstead.*)

Sal. I killed the ukulele.

Will that do?

Can I stop now?

Please?

Come on, Sally, let me quit now.

I'm beggin you. What's my name? Just say what my name is. You don't have to call me darling with it, but just say that one thing. Say my name.

Once.

A
CEREMONY
FOR THE
MIDGET

Henry Rector, owner of the Midget Bar and Grill in Key Bonita, suffered two kinds of bad luck at once: his business went bad and his wife turned sour on him.

During the heyday of the Midget you would have found people packed into the little place cheek by jowl on almost any night of the week. Even on the dreariest Monday when great barnlike emporiums on the same waterfront street had to rob their own cash registers to feed their jukeboxes, the Midget served up drinks to every table. Seafaring persons seemed to be drawn to the close animal proximity forced on them by the smallness of the place. And then, too, these men had enjoyed the presence of Henry Rector's blond wife, Consilada.

This trim and pretty woman with her sweet, blue-eyed smile had been a real drawing card. She went about her business in the place with the air of a child who had not yet lost its knowledge of angels; there was some fragile expectancy in her mood that made each man feel he had been created for the express purpose of protecting her from disappointments.

But then through some unhappy transformation she became nothing but the greater portion of Henry Rector's bad luck. At first, right along with the decline of the Midget, as if keeping pace with it, there developed in her

171

temperament a certain sharpness that was at times down-right strident and ugly. She began to say peculiar things and laid claim to crazy visions; and when someone dis-believed her she would turn on him like a nasty, yapping little dog. Soon she began to use bad language and to pick fights with old customers and with Henry himself, and before long her sweet smile was a forgotten thing in that saloon. Consilada Rector became known instead for the deep crease between her eyes, and all that blue color went for nothing; her mouth, too, became awful, a little red per-simmon of sarcasm and derision.

Henry told her she was driving all the trade away with her behavior. But he never once gave voice to his deepest fear, that Consilada would one day drive him away, too.

And then at last, on a gloomy, deadly still summer night in the second year of the Midget's decline, all of his troubles came to a head at once and the poor man was forced to tack this note to the front door of his saloon:

CLOSED FOR GOOD. AM GOING TO WORK LAYING BLOCK ON MONDAY MORNING. SOUVENIERS OF THE MIDGET GIVEN OUT FREE ON SUNDAY AT 4 IN THE AFT.

HENRY RECTOR

Then he opened the door again and called to his wife, who was seated on a stool at the end of the bar. "You coming with me, Consilada?"

"Thank you, Henry," she said coldly, "I'll just set here for a while, if you please."

Henry waited for a moment at the door, and then he went inside and stood next to her. He was as big as Consilada was small: his biceps measured only a few inches less than her waistline. He had a good, big, open face with gentle dark brown eyes and a head of thick smoke-colored hair. His voice when he spoke to Consilada was pitched much lower than at other times: this was an effort to control the trembling in it that was caused by his love for her.

"Take a drive up the Keys?" he said. "Let the wind blow in that pretty yellow hair?"

Consilada turned her eyes toward him but she did not raise them to his face. "I believe I said I'd just set here a-while. Or did I merely imagine I said that?" Then she thrust her eyes at him like a pair of deadly blue knives. "Now why can't you get out of here and leave me alone?"

At daybreak, Consilada Rector was still perched on that stool at the end of the bar, alone. Twice in the night she had gone to the ladies' room to repair her makeup and each time returned to the same stool to continue what was, in all respects, a vigil of the utmost importance to her. At certain intervals she would have the jukebox going, but more often the place was silent as a conch shell except for the small noises Consilada herself created. Along toward noon she was surprised by a sudden drowsiness and fought it off with a glass of cognac.

And then, at a certain moment in the middle of the afternoon, it became clear to her that the vigil was nearing its end. The saloon was invaded by an unearthly almost palpable tension that caused her heart to quicken in a painful way. She began to behave like a desperate woman whose indifferent lover may enter the room at any second: tossed quick anxious smiles at the bar mirror and got no comfort from it whatever. She tried to relax with a deep studied breathing that did no good at all. Once, she looked down and found her own hand vigorously caressing her stomach as if to quiet the yowling of some anxious creature deep in her womb.

From time to time, as if she were trying to surprise someone in the act of spying on her, the little blonde's eyes, glistening with expectation, would dart into some shadowy corner of the saloon; and often they came to rest in a certain patch of darkness surrounding the jukebox. She seemed to be awaiting the arrival of a kind of being who might emerge from almost anywhere, or from nowhere at all.

At about four o'clock in the afternoon, she heard a key turning in the front door lock. Her body went limp with dismay. For a moment the saloon was flooded with shrill afternoon light; and then the door closed again, restoring a sense of twilight to the place.

The blonde did not even look up. She knew her husband had returned. He laid an enormous hand on her hip. She stiffened, but still he left the hand there.

"Consilada?" he said.

After a moment, she turned to face him. "Henry. Please. Go with that long face. Just go. We don't need that long face."

"You spend the whole night in here?"

"Nor any complaining," she said.

"You staying again tonight?" he asked.

"I might and I might not."

"They're tearing it all out of here starting Monday," he said. "What you going to do then, Consilada?"

"*Today*, do you mind if I don't answer petty questions, Henry? Today me and the Midget like to pretend nobody hates us."

"You know I don't hate you neither one. All I been talking was in my opinion the Midget is a mere saloon."

"Oh, I heard you, Henry. And how you think that makes me look? Like a jackass would you say? Or a nut?" She looked down at the hand on her hip. "You suppose I could get that hand moved, please?"

Henry took the hand away and with a slow, lumbering stride he walked to the other end of the bar and sat down.

"I'm simpleminded, Consilada," he said, looking at her image in the mirror. "I'm a country boy. I say the Midget is a mere goddam saloon. Everybody comes in here says the same thing."

"You know what *I* say, Henry? I say your mouth is as smart as your big feet."

Henry took a bottle of whiskey from his jacket pocket and drank from it.

Consilada lighted a cigarette.

Both their eyes were focused on the one image: hers, in the mirror.

After a moment there was a rap on the door. They both shouted *Come in,* and a second couple entered the place. The woman was about forty, plain and plump. Her face was painted, but her hair was still in curlers. The man was slender, wiry, slit-mouthed, as plain as his wife.

Consilada glanced quickly toward the door. "Oh. It's you."

The man and woman looked at one another, and shrugged. Then the man sat next to Henry, and Henry gave him the bottle to drink from.

The woman walked over to Consilada, but she did not sit down.

" 'Oh,' " she mimicked, " '*it's you.*' "

"Hello," Consilada said.

"Look, Consilada," the woman said. "I am here to attend a party for the closing of the Midget."

"I appreciate it, Patti. The *Midget* appreciates it."

"However," Patti said, hands on her hips, "I am not worth a damn at *funerals.*"

"It's not going to be a funeral," Consilada said.

"I didn't even go to my father's. In fact, I'd have left *town* to get out of it! That's how I stand on funerals."

"They's not going to be any damn funeral, so shut up!"

Patti said, "Maybe you want me go back home *altogether?*"

"My!" Consilada said. "Aren't you touchy today! What's the matter, you having a touchy day today? Whew!"

The plump woman pursed her lips, and sat on the stool next to the owner of the bankrupt saloon. "Oh, Consilada, don't be like this. We come to help close the place for godsake. Is this the way you want to close the Midget? Now give me a ciggie and behave."

Patti took a cigarette from the packet on the counter. Before lighting it, she leaned in toward Consilada, and said in a small voice, "He been around today, Con?"

Consilada said, "He's not *showing* himself, I can tell you. He won't show himself to hatred." She glanced toward Henry to indicate her meaning, and then back to Patti. "But he's *here* all right."

Patti stole a quick look at the jukebox, and then she shivered and lighted her cigarette. The two women smoked in silence for a moment.

"John," said Henry, to the man sitting next to him at the other end of the bar, "the world is got two camps in it: *one* is thousands of people't say the Midget is a goddam saloon, and th'other camp made up of one woman alone named Consilada Rector. This Consilada Rector been claiming for two years now the Midget is a *person*. Which is all right her thinking so, John, but she can't shut up on the topic. Thus we got a situation where everybody boy-cotts the Midget *saloon*."

Consilada did not look at her husband. She turned to her friend. "Oh, Patti, I'm so glad ever since I got this ear condition where I have trouble hearing certain things. You don't know what a pleasure it is, that when a certain tone of voice talks, you just don't *hear* it!"

"And," continued Henry, as if he had not been inter-rupted at all, "for what reason is it the Midget is getting boycotted? Simply so people don't have to come in here and listen about the Midget *person,* which can't be seen. And the sweet result, John? We can't renew the license, and tomorrow morning I go to work laying block."

"I can't explain it *exactly*, Patti," said Consilada. "It's just a certain *pitch*, like say, hatred, which my ears just don't hear a thing. You don't know what a thrill that is."

"Now, John," said the big man at the other end of the bar, "I always claimed it was possible for a person to talk the'self right to the poorhouse. And what we getting here is a living example of just that."

Consilada tapped the bar with her fingernails. She smiled at her friend, a tight-mouthed, icy smile. "All I wanted to do in the world," she said, "was have a little ceremony, a ceremony for the closing of the Midget. And boy, aren't I catching hell for it?"

"Oh, Consilada," Patti said, "now you two *quit*."

"The Midget been operating here twelve years, and *I* know I'm a damn fool, but it seemed to me like there ought to be some little *do!*"

"I agree, I *agree*," said Patti.

"You don't have to humor me." Consilada started to cry. Patti put her hand on Consilada's shoulder.

Henry said, "John, you see that little blawnd woman at the end of the bar there? The one weeping? I get the impression what she wants is some kind of a ceremony or other. Isn't that what you get, that impression?" John kept his mouth strictly shut, and Henry continued: "I just wonder what that little blawnd woman thinks is been going *on* in here this last twelve years.

"In 1947 alone, we had two stabbings. In 1949, the boys from the *Katydid* staged a full-scale war in here, killed one United States sailor from the U.S. Navy and got us put off limits for six months. In 1953, on a Saturday night, a pregnit woman come in here, waltzed on back to the phone booth and give birth to a nine-pound bastard. Drew such a crowd, had to lock the front door. My point is, if that little blawnd woman don't think we had enough *ceremony* yet, what is it she thinks been going on in here for twelve years?"

Patti hoisted herself up, with her feet on the rail, and looked past Consilada down to the end of the bar where the men were sitting. "Henry, you talking about Annie Lou? Annie Lou made that boy a good mother, Henry. And don't forget who was practically the midwife, now, won't you? It was *me*." She pointed at herself. "Me, right here."

Henry acknowledged this detail by pointing his thumb toward Patti. "She was practically the midwife," he said.

Patti sat down again, stared wide-eyed into the mirror over the bar. "Gosh, all the *times* in here!" she said. "Just gosh, is all I can say. Just gosh, gosh, gosh." Then she turned to Consilada: "Where's Fitch and Martha?"

"*I* don't know."

"And all the shrimpers?"

"*I* don't know."

"The Thompsons and Dolores and Kookie and them?"

"I don't *know!*"

"You mean," Patti said, "me and John are *it?*"

"You're it."

"Well, you can count on me to tell them Thompsons a thing or two."

"Ah, frig 'em," said Consilada.

"You're right, you're right!"

"You see, Patti, it was no mere accident." Consilada pointed a thumb in the direction of her husband. "It was *him* put the finish on this party."

Henry's hand closed tight around the whiskey bottle he had been drinking from.

Consilada said, "I let it be known far and wide, for godsake. Kids, I said, I'm handing out free glasses from the Midget on Sunday afternoon. Souvenirs, I said, of all the crazy trips to the moon in this place."

She rose from the stool and walked over to one of the tables. "Everything else is being impounded, the counter, all the equipment, every damn thing, even that stool you got your butt on." She picked up a carton from the table and carried it back to the bar with her. "But these glasses I held out for souvenirs. Of course, nobody *wants* the damn things."

Consilada took one of the glasses, smiled at it and held it next to her cheek. "Oh, Patti, honey, you'll take one, won't you, one little glass?"

"*Course,* tickled to death!"

Consilada handed over the glass, tenderly. "There, a glass from the Midget, with his compliments, full to the brim with the world's rarest liquor."

Patti tilted the glass and blinked at the emptiness. She looked with arched brows at Consilada: "Full, huh?"

"Right to the brim. Smell it."

"Oh, yeah. *Sensational.*"

"Y'see," Consilada explained, "the way they make liquor is they distill it. Now you take all the things has happened in here in twelve years: the meeting of you and John, all the fallings in love that's gone on in here, all the laughing and all the secrets been told, et cetera—and you *distill* it. Do you follow me? That's the kind of liquor *my* midget brewed."

Patti smiled sympathetically. Then she said, "Hey, Con, all kidding aside, you got anything to put in here?"

The little blond woman looked at her plump friend with horror and disbelief.

Patti said, "I mean in the way of liquor."

"*Give* me that glass!" Consilada breathed.

The glass was returned to her. She lifted it, and without turning her eyes from Patti's she smashed it against the far wall of the place. "*You,*" she said, her mouth uglied by a downward turning at the corners. "*You didn't hear a word I said.*"

Patti looked at Consilada for a moment; then she rose from the stool and grabbed her pocketbook. "All right, that's it, that's it! *That is it!*"

Enraged, she pranced toward the door. "Come on, John. There's a crazy woman loose. Shall we just *leave?*"

Henry put a hand on John's arm. "If you sit tight, John, you might yet see a little ceremony in here today."

John remained on his stool, and the men helped themselves to another swallow of whiskey.

The women faced each other across the saloon.

"Thank you, Miss Patti," said Consilada, with a slight smile in her voice. "For showing your true colors."

"*My true what?*"

"Colors. Your true colors."

"Meaning! Exactly! What!"

"Oh, nothing." Consilada spoke softly. "It's just that I been operating this Midget Bar for twelve years here, behaving like a saint. Other people come in and they have killings, they fall in love all over the place, they birth their goddam babies in my phone booth. They just suit theirselves. But what happens when *I* cut loose for once and break a thirty-two-cent glass? Everybody turns on me like a snake. Now shut up and have a little Seagram's."

Patti just stood there for a moment, her mouth and eyes wide open.

Consilada said, "Well? D'you want a little Seagram's?"

"No," Patti said, "I don't want a little Seagram's. I want a *lot* of it." She returned to the bar and plunked down onto the stool, worn out.

Consilada said, "I just thought, they's a *few* people in the world you can show a true feeling to, and Patti's one." She poured a drink of whiskey and handed it to her friend. "So if I was out o' line there, I'm *sorry!*"

Then she poured a drink for herself and sat next to Patti.

There was a tense silence in the place for a while. Little meaningful glances were exchanged between the women, and others between the men. These glances seemed to acknowledge the tension each of them felt.

Consilada was the first to speak. "Just talking along general lines, Patti, it's a fact that a man can't stand to hear about a thing unless he can lay a big hammy hand on it."

"I know, honey, I know," Patti whispered. "But *sssh*, just *sssh* now."

"Like, take a woman's butt," Consilada said. "There's something a man can lay a big hammy hand on it, see? So that's fine. Only if that woman happens to have a friend, even one little weensy friend that he can't *see*, then Christ help her!"

"Now, Con, look," Patti said, "the way I am with me and John: I figure he's a man, I'm a woman, so what the hell. See what I mean? Now quit it, honey."

"Oh, I'm only talking along very general lines here," Consilada said. "For instance, if he can't take me as I am, let him *push off*. Who needs it. I'm sorry."

"I'd hate you kids to bust up over this," Patti said. "Listen, I'm going over there and talk to him for a minute."

Consilada raised her small white shoulders. "*Forget* it. Just hang onto your oxygen. He never hears nothing."

Patti moistened her lips and lowered herself from the stool. She walked right over to Henry's end of the bar.

"Henry, can I put in a word? And you shut up, John, right?"

The men nodded agreement to both proposals.

"Well, it's this, Henry," she began. "When my daddy died, I didn't go to the funeral, right?"

The big man looked at her. "What's that got to do, Patti?"

"Nothing," she said, "just that I chose between the living and the dead. John here was the living, so I didn't go to the funeral of my daddy, which was the dead. I'm telling you something, Henry."

"Go on tell me."

"All right, here's my point. Two weeks after his funeral, which I didn't go to, *my daddy come into my bedroom at the Gulfstream.* And he set on the edge of my bed. Now that's my only point I'm trying to make."

"I'm tickled to hear it, Patti. But was you running a saloon in your bedroom?"

"No, I wasn't. I was just making a point. You get my point?"

"Because in saloons," Henry said, "is where people don't want to sit drinking with that kind of talk."

"Henry, please," Patti said. "My point is, I didn't *invite* my daddy. He just come there anyway on his own *accord.* You see my point now?"

"What they want in a saloon," Henry continued, "is people they can pinch, and feel is still warm. Otherwise they stay home to the Gulfstream and talk to they dead daddies on the edge of the bed."

Patti made fists and placed them on her hips. "Oh, *shoot,* Henry! You just don't listen to a person atoll!"

She went back to Consilada, waving her hands as if something nasty had got on them. "I give up."

When she had climbed back onto her stool, she found Consilada looking at her in a peculiar, thin-lipped way.

"Well, I tried, honey," she began to explain.

"Yes," the little blonde interrupted her. "I *heard* you try!"

"Well?"

"You," Consilada said, "you been trying all this time to make people think the Midget is a *ghost!*"

"Well, isn't that the *i*-dea?"

"And *you* are my best friend!"

"Consilada. What the living hell do you want from a friend, honey, hmmm?"

"*Understanding!*" snarled Consilada.

Patti said, "Oh, lord." Then she turned away, scratched

her head, tried to yawn and ended up whistling. She rose from the stool and moved across the floor, snapping out a beat with her fingers. "Miss Consi-*la*-da," she sang, "if they's gonna be a *ceremony*, I'd say it was damn near *time* for it."

Consilada turned and lowered her head, looking at the dancing woman through narrowed eyes until all movement of any kind had ceased entirely. Then she said, "There's not gonna be any."

"John," said Patti, "there's not gonna be any. Y'hear? So come on, for godsake."

John looked to Henry for a gesture of dismissal. Henry winked at him and nodded. Then John rose and joined the woman at the door.

Patti had one hand on the lock as she said, "Consilada, I just pray when the day comes, it won't be too late. Because the day is coming."

"*What* day?" Consilada challenged.

"The day you need your friends."

Consilada turned her eyes to the mirror over the bar. "God spare me," she said, praying to her own image, "God spare me from my friends. God spare me from the human race."

"Careful what you pray for, hon. You might get it."

As Patti and John went out the door, there was a quick flood of harsh daylight in the saloon.

Then, in the semidarkness of the place, the husband and the wife, at opposite ends of the bar, sat for a moment in silence, each of them studying the woman's image in the mirror.

The man said, "Consilada?"

The woman gave no sign of having heard him.

"I'm crazy about you, Consilada."

The woman ground out her cigarette. "Oh, goody," she said.

The man got slowly to his feet and walked down to the end of the bar where his wife was seated. As he approached she stiffened and said, "Don't touch me."

"I won't touch you, Consilada."

He picked up the carton of glasses and took a few steps backward, away from the bar. Then he raised the carton with both arms and threw it directly at the woman's image in the mirror.

There were two crashes at once: the smaller one of the highball glasses breaking, like the tinkling of a thousand Japanese chimes, and the more substantial clatter of thick mirror fragments falling to the floor.

The woman did not allow herself to react. Her body remained stiff, her face immobile.

The man said, "That was a ceremony, Consilada." Then he lumbered slowly to the door, and left the place.

Consilada breathed deeply. Then, starting at her neck, she ran the fingers of both hands up through her hair, and shook her head back and forth. She opened her pocketbook and took out a small vanity case; and when she had adjusted her appearance, the woman rose from the stool and started around the bar to survey the damage. But she was stopped midway by a small reedy voice that said, "Hee-hee."

Consilada spun around and saw the Midget: a tiny, handsome creature of indeterminate age, wearing a moss-green suit, a black bow tie, and a jaunty black fedora. He was perched on the jukebox, legs crossed, smiling. His eyes were big, wide-open, noncommittal: they simply looked at her.

The woman started toward him, head high, arms outstretched, walking with all the grace she could muster, trying hard not to run. As she approached, the Midget waved a forefinger back and forth, and said, "Mustn't touch, remember?"

Consilada stood before him, a large woman now, in contrast with the Midget. Her brow was furrowed with longing. She placed her hands behind her back, torturing her own fingers. "I'll bet you're sore," she said, "about the ceremony."

The Midget shook his head. "You couldn't be more mistaken. I *loved* it."

Still smiling his say-nothing smile, he tapped the coin slot with the toe of his tiny, patent-leather shoe. "Now, why don't you play something snappy, and see if you can keep time with the broom."

And he pointed a slim, elegant finger toward the mess of shattered glass behind the bar.

SWEET
WILLIAM

Miss Anna was embarrassed at the way her son behaved at his father's funeral: he was all smiles. And she thought his suit, which had looked dark enough in the closet, was altogether too bright a blue for the occasion. But nobody'd blame her for that: in 1933, you wore what you had.

Leaving the church, she nudged him with her elbow and motioned him to lean down for a message. William was the tallest seventeen-year-old in Key West, and since Miss Anna was such a tiny thing, he nearly bent over double to hear what she had to say:

"You can just nod at your friends, William, you don't have to grin like that. In fact, a little frown wouldn't hurt."

From then on, he did fairly well by her, considering it was his favorite day in memory. But once, during a delay at graveside—the coffin was late—William took out his jew's harp and got through three bars of "De Camptown Races" before Miss Anna could reach up and grab it away from his face. This little episode caused some of the other mourners to swell up and hold their breaths, while others let out their laughter by pretending to have coughing fits.

Miss Anna finally gave up; there was no changing the nature of the occasion. It was a happy funeral and that's all there was to it.

No one present could remember a single event in Bull Bramer's life that had given more pleasure to others than his death.

He'd been sitting in a saloon listening to a baseball game over the radio. As the winning run was scored by the Detroit Tigers, the old man, who'd bet twenty-five cents on the White Sox, roared out a stream of oaths and fell off his stool. The bartender had looked him over to be certain his pulse had stopped, then announced that Bull Bramer had just dropped dead to save a quarter.

The widow heard the story too, and if it failed to amuse her, it was not owing to any disapproval of its levity. She herself was delighted to see in his grave a man who had abused her William so scandalously. (Once—a typical stunt—he'd wrapped the boy in a fishnet and left him hanging from a tree the better part of an afternoon, going out every now and then to turn the hose on him.) The seriousness of her own mood had quite another cause: the sudden cessation of Bull Bramer's seven-dollar-a-week pay envelope.

On the evening of that very day, Miss Anna spoke to William about money.

Even though she herself had a special fondness for it, claimed there was never enough of it, and always smiled when it came at her out of the blue, Miss Anna felt she had failed somehow to instill in her son a proper respect for it. As a small boy, when he was first learning the clink and the jangle and the weight and the shine of it, he'd liked it well enough. But its power never got hold of his imagination as it does most other children's. He found it a nuisance: if you hung upside down on a branch it fell out of your pocket, if you went swimming you had to hold it in your mouth and the taste was bitter. After a while, he'd given up fooling with it.

But now, on the night of the funeral, sitting in her rocker on the front porch, Miss Anna explained that things were apt to be harder for him now than what they had been before.

William thought he could tell by the way she played with her lower lip, twiddling it between her thumb and forefinger as she spoke, that the situation was fairly urgent.

But he was mistaken. Miss Anna had plenty of money. She owned the house there on China Lane, was about to collect on Bull Bramer's insurance, and had secret bank accounts in Tampa to boot. Her playing with her lip was caused by thinking how much she had, not how little; the two situations often provoke a similar agitation in money lovers.

"The way I see it, William, you're six foot two and a half, your daddy's dead, and nursing jobs is rare as hen's teeth. These days people nurse their own. So that lets me out, I'm not good for a nickel. But I figure with you being six foot two and a half . . ."

Miss Anna talked on and on that night, worrying the situation to death, apparently taking into account neither William's considerable gifts nor his extraordinary popularity.

There wasn't a storekeeper in Key West who wouldn't have tried to make a place for William on his payroll. All over town they welcomed his loose-jointed, lighthearted presence, the oddly pretty, off-key music of his jew's harp, the glow of goodness in his long, open face.

Nor was his presence merely pleasant; the boy was useful as well. Perhaps the quality he was most noted for was his effect on mad dogs and crying babies: no ugly beast was ever known to bark at him, not even in August, but more than one had shut up at the sight of him and come over to lick his hand. A mother with a bawling infant or a cantankerous small child breathed a sigh of relief if she saw William coming up her lane. They all claimed it was worth a dozen nipples just to have him there, somewhere in the general area of the commotion. For within a moment or two, the screaming would cease, and when he walked away, he left behind him some special silence and the air all infected with sweetness.

He also had a natural gift for fixing things. This was appreciated especially by fisherman. William's fingers were as nimble as they were long, he could restore to usefulness old nets that had seemed no better than a hopeless mess of worn-out ropes.

In no time at all, William was working six days a week at the boatyard. Previously each fisherman had mended his own nets, but William was twice as fast at it, did a better job, and charged practically nothing. He also did scraping and painting and all manner of general fixing, and soon had as much work as he could handle.

For a long time life was good.

The Bramers kept a few chickens, raised bananas and Key limes right in their own yard, and there was always a splendid fish for the table whenever it was wanted, a big red snapper or a grouper or some other luscious sea-thing William'd bring home free. His mother was a good cook and they ate like a couple of bishops.

Especially Miss Anna. In the months following her husband's death she gradually took to gorging herself. The way she packed it away, you'd have thought the stuff was drawing interest at some colossal rate. In no time at all she'd eaten herself into the shape of a happy little pink ball. But still she went right on taking her place in the breadlines to get the flour and sugar and beans Franklin Roosevelt was passing out.

As for William, he was learning about tiredness and backaches and all the various pains that came with hard work. But each evening at suppertime he left the fishing pier at a great pace, hurrying toward the thrill of lighting up Miss Anna's face with his handful of coins. There is no keener joy for a man than the joy of pleasing a woman, and William never got enough of it. Her delight warmed him like rum and he even savored the afterglow: sitting on a stool he'd watch as she waddled about the kitchen tasting and testing and poking at things with forks and chattering about nothing at all, still clearly enchanted by the lovely new jangle he'd brought to her apron pocket.

Now and then, too, like a surprise taste of candy would come the thought of his father, all nailed up in his box over at the bone orchard, no longer in a condition to make misery for anyone. But that was only for the first few months. The past seemed to have little hold on him. Within a year it was as if Bull Bramer had never existed, and life had always and always and always had this new shape: just the two of them, him and his beloved, plump little mama.

And then one evening, which was in the seventh year of this fine new time, certain puzzling words were spoken in the Bramer kitchen, and everything began to change.

Dr. MacMurtree was there for supper. He was Miss Anna's oldest friend, he had attended at William's birth, and in the old days when she'd done home nursing, most of her cases had been his patients. Now that his wife was gone, this kindly man took an occasional evening meal with the Bramers.

On this night of the puzzling words, the doctor folded his napkin neatly, belched deep and long with his mouth wide-open, and said:

"You got that room ready, Miss Anna?"

He was a tall, high-strung, overworked man who loved good food and always belched after supper. He was in his seventies now, but you could still see clearly what the doctor's appearance had been as a boy. His hair had turned white but it was still thick and cowlicked front and back same as ever, and his Adam's apple looked like new.

Miss Anna glanced furtively at William before answering Dr. MacMurtree's question. "Yes," she said. Then she tittered nervously and added, "Oh yes," leaving William entirely in the dark.

William's eyes grew larger, but he said nothing.

Some days earlier, he'd heard Miss Anna moving about in the spare room upstairs. Later, he saw that she'd opened the windows and put a clean counterpane on the bed, but at the time he'd attached no importance to the matter.

Even when Dr. MacMurtree had gone home and he and Miss Anna were sitting in their wicker chairs on the front porch, William noticed she was doing a good deal of lip-twiddling. But she said nothing. Once, because their eyes met, Miss Anna made an odd little sound, something like laughter. But it wasn't laughter. And then she went to bed.

The next morning at breakfast, they heard the ambulance stop out front. Miss Anna got up from the table so fast she spilled coffee all down her front. Only then did William notice she was wearing one of her white nurse's uniforms.

He went out front to watch what happened next: two men in white opened the back door of the ambulance. Miss Anna said something to them and then went back up onto the porch, not once looking at William. She held the screen door open as the attendants carried something past her and up the stairs to the spare room.

After the first glance, William avoided looking at the thing directly. It was probably a person since it had that general shape, but hovering all about it was a damp sheath of ugly light, a kind of upside-down light that gave off darkness instead of illumination. Not wanting to go back into the house, he wandered off in the direction of the docks.

Somewhere in his memory was a similar thing, a thing of a like shape and character, and he racked his brain trying to remember what that long-ago thing had been. Later in the morning, he was surprised to find himself on a scaffold at the boatyard with a wire brush in his hand, scraping dead paint from the hull of an old fishing boat. William was unaccustomed to rummaging around in the bottom of his mind, looking for the faces of ugly lost things. It was like being in two places at once and all day long he kept going back and forth from where he was to where he wasn't.

At suppertime, he walked home slowly, stopping at every opportunity to use up minutes with visiting, anything at all that would delay his arrival.

He entered China Lane at that soft middle moment of twilight, the time of evening when the sun has stopped casting hard shadows and a person is most apt to be surprised by the beauty of familiar things.

William stood still, just looking: saw the coconut trees, the dark pink blossoms of oleander, all the other green things and flowering bushes; saw the sand-colored ground, the chicken coop with its nightly flutter of white and red caused by his own nearness to wing and comb (all part of the wonder of being William; your fame was known even among the fowls); saw the cottage itself, its old gray boards rich with weather, saw the light in the kitchen window, a warmer amber for his mother's presence at the stove and all the good aromas she sent forth from it. He looked at it all once and he looked at it all again, and then he felt the pain that comes from seeing such splendor and knowing yourself to be a part of it.

In his head he had begun to hear a certain song. He took the jew's harp from his pocket, intending to give the melody some accompaniment, when an unusual thing happened: he shivered. The instrument felt cold against his teeth.

At that moment William remembered what it was that had frightened him all day, saw once again the face of the old dread he'd been searching for since breakfast.

He went around to the back and called softly to his mother through the kitchen door.

Miss Anna came out onto the back stoop, absently licking something from her fingers. "William?" She saw him standing under the fig tree some few yards from the house. "William, why you standing over there like that?"

He motioned to her with his hand. Miss Anna walked over and stood next to him. "What is it, son?"

"Mama," he whispered, looking at the light in the upstairs bedroom window. "Have you got Bull Bramer up there again?"

She made an awful face. "Oh! Oh, William! What an *i*-dea!"

"Tell me."

"Oh, son! Is that what you worried about? Heavens above, your father is dead. Don't you 'member? How we buried him and all?"

"Maybe so, but all I want to know is, is he in there?"

Miss Anna put her hand on William's arm. "No. No, he's not in there. It's Mr. Bolts in there. Mr. Bolts is our new patient."

William felt some relief, but he continued to look at her carefully as she spoke.

"If I'd've told you beforehand, you wouldn't've liked the *i*-dea. But I figured, after you met him, saw what a darlin' old gentleman he is, you'd be real glad. Anyway, it'll only be for a couple weeks." She spoke the next words so softly her voice was hardly audible. "He's gonna die. Hadden got more'n two weeks to live."

Miss Anna then explained that Dr. MacMurtree had begged her to help him out with this one case, a poor old bachelor who had no place to go and die. She said she'd found the plea so touching it was impossible to refuse.

Miss Anna judged it best not to mention to William certain other facts of Mr. Bolts's history: his sister in Naples had taken him into her own home in the spring with the strict understanding that he was to die at once. However, after keeping him for a month, the sister had been under sedation ever since while Mr. Bolts had not only refrained from dying but had behaved in such a way as to get himself turned out of five different nursing homes, lasting less than a week in four of them. The fifth had endured him for more than a month but Mr. Bolts swore they'd kept him in a locked room bound and gagged most of the time. Now, for the luxury of having him out of town altogether—and unable to find a place in Naples that would take him in— this desperate woman was offering double the usual rate for home-care cases. This circumstance might well have been the one to touch Miss Anna so deeply she found herself unable to refuse. But surely one further aspect of the situation would have moved her to accept him even if the lure of double compensation had failed:

It had been arranged with a lawyer that one thousand dollars would be paid to Miss Anna on the occasion of Mr. Bolts's death. In exchange for this sum, the woman in Naples was to have the assurance that she would not hear her brother's name spoken until the time came to arrange for the disposition of his body.

Miss Anna, after accepting the proposal, invented a myth about herself: that she had a special touch with difficult patients. There was no truth to it, however. Cranky people scared her half to death. But the myth did serve to comfort her, at least for a day or two.

"Now come on in, William," she said, "and say hello to the poor old thing." She took him by the hand and led him into the house. At the foot of the stairs, she stopped and whispered, "Only thing you got to look out for is Mr. Bolts's sense of humor. It's real *dry*. Know what I mean?"

She led the way up the stairs to Bull Bramer's old room, knocked softly on the door and opened it.

Mr. Bolts was propped up on pillows, leaning against the iron bedstead, reading a magazine called *Wild West*. The cover illustration was of an Indian in the act of scalping a yellow-haired girl.

Mr. Bolts himself had no hair at all. His head was huge and gray and shiny and the only thing on it was glasses. He had as many frowns as it is possible to fit into one face: a large one between his eyes, with several smaller ones at either side, and the lines at the corner of his mouth gave the impression that the mouth itself was a kind of horizontal frown. This was also true of his neck; each of those old creases seemed to be expressing displeasure.

"Mr. Bolts, guess who's here to say hello!" Miss Anna's voice was full of cheer, but the man on the bed did not lift his eyes from the magazine.

"Shut up," he said. His voice was a harsh rasp that hurt the throat of the listener. He turned the page and went on reading, moving his lips with each word.

Miss Anna laughed, using just her face and making no sound at all, and whispered to William, "He's such a character, you're gonna be crazy about him."

At length, Mr. Bolts looked at William over the top of the magazine.

"Crouch!" he said. "Make him crouch! I can't stand tallness!"

William looked at Miss Anna, wondering what was expected of him.

Miss Anna shook her own shoulders and moved her face about, acting out mirth. "You want him to crouch, Mr. Bolts? You mean crouch down like this?" She bent her knees, putting her hands on her thighs for support.

"That's what crouch means," Mr. Bolts rasped. "Everybody knows what crouch means."

"William," she said, still smiling, making a game of it, "would you crouch for Mr. Bolts?"

William crouched.

Mr. Bolts looked at him for a long time, obviously displeased with what he saw.

"Why don't he talk? Is they something wrong with him?"

"Oh, he can talk real good. Say something, William. Go ahead."

William, still crouching, said, "How do, sir."

"How do what?" said Mr. Bolts.

"Just how do, I guess," said William, not knowing what to say.

Mr. Bolts took up his magazine again, keeping his eyes on it as he turned the page and said, "Keep him out o' here. Don't like the way he looks at me."

The old, sweet days were gone from China Lane. Within a week, there was hardly a sign of them.

When William came home in the evening he would find Miss Anna perspiring and out of breath and with a wild, frightened, distracted look in her eye. Their long happy suppers were a thing of the past. Miss Anna took her meals on the run, a bite here and a sip there between trips to the sickroom. The food was superb and Mr. Bolts ate vast quantities of it, at least three times the amount he was allowed, but still he complained of it and always demanded a number of adjustments. If he found the temperature to his taste, then the helping was either too small or too large, or it had been served on an unsuitable plate. And like the servant of a king, Miss Anna had to stand there in his presence and sample each dish for poison.

There was no longer any porch-sitting in the evenings. She took her rest in brief snatches, leaning against a wall or a doorway, and at night she slept with one eye open, and very little at that. For the clatter of cowbells (he had three and rang them all at once) shattered every dream. And it would be followed by shouts of "*Slop jar!*" or "*Bedpan!*" Miss Anna would struggle into her robe, hurrying to quiet him before the noise had awakened all of China Lane. And there was never any real emergency to attend to. After as long as ten or fifteen minutes of waiting, "I changed my mind," he would say. "Couldn't I just leave it here for you?" Miss Anna had suggested. But no, he claimed he couldn't tolerate the sight of porcelain objects staring at him all night long, and snarled at her offer to make a "pretty little cloth cover for it." In any event, his personal habits were such that the bed linens had to be changed a number of times each day; but these porcelain articles he found so offensive—even while he was unable to pass a night without their being brought to his side—remained as white as virginal souls.

William kept away from the sickroom. On Sundays, while Miss Anna was at chuch, he sat in attendance on the front porch, but Mr. Bolts made it a point never to ring his bells at those times.

Even though there was no actual contact between the two men, Mr. Bolts was forever complaining of abuses he suffered at William's hands. Often in the mornings he claimed the jew's harp had kept him awake all night long, but Miss Anna knew William had ceased playing it—except perhaps when he went downtown in the evenings, which he did more and more frequently as the days grew into weeks.

And Mr. Bolts swore that William crept into his room at night to steal things. Later the missing article would be found hidden under his pillows or among the bedclothes.

Miss Anna had of course long since abandoned her pathetic efforts to attribute Mr. Bolts's behavior to a sense of humor. She now called it his "death agony," said she knew this to be a familiar thing in the dying; they were desperate for all the human attention they could get, for it would be their last.

Her patience seemed awesome, but the fact was that she had been hypnotized by the image of the money. She saw the thousand dollars in cash, denominations of one, ten stacks of a hundred each, and the green was the deep shiny green of young aralia leaves.

But would she ever get her hands on it? Mr. Bolts showed no sign of dying. Dr. MacMurtree kept assuring her that such asthmatic old lungs were worthless and the heart wasn't worth a damn either; any day now, he claimed, one or both would give out. But as the weeks wore on, the doctor shook his head in awe at such staying power, the terrible old man wheezed with glee at his own survival, and Miss Anna wondered if ever again she would hear the music of William's jew's harp.

For her son had fallen into a kind of somnambulism that caused her much anguish. There'd been no rain for weeks, August had been still as death, and time just seemed to hang in the air like so much bitter fruit on a tree no one went near. It was easy to tell herself William's mood was only a summer complaint. But in her heart she knew better, she knew no amount of weather could work such evil on them.

Once, considering William's terrible new sadness, she was on the point of telling Dr. MacMurtree to have the old cuss hauled out of her house at once.

But what if they took Mr. Bolts somewhere else and he died after only a day or two? Such a thing could easily happen, and if it did her regret would be so great and profound and poisonous she wasn't at all certain of her ability to hold up under it.

Meanwhile, one September midnight, William became aware that something peculiar was happening to the house itself.

He'd been sitting with friends at the Cuban ice-cream parlor on Duval Street, and on this particular evening, he'd found himself more reluctant to leave than ever before and had stayed on till the place closed.

Going home at last, he walked down China Lane, stopping in front of the house for a long while, just looking, not even knowing the reason for his hesitation. And quite suddenly he began to see the change:

The entire house had taken on the aspect of Mr. Bolts.

The windows were no longer simply open; they stared at him now in a disagreeable way, and the breeze that blew the curtains moved in petulant little gusts. The old deck planks on the front porch had cracks between them from which something unpleasant was being exhaled, a kind of sourness that rose and formed an invisible curtain through which one had to pass in order to enter the house.

William had no doubt about the reality of what he beheld. One good look was all he needed.

He spent that night on the deck of the *Marilu*. She was in drydock under a stand of coconut trees at the edge of the boatyard. Using a pile of ropes for a pillow, he had his first undisturbed sleep of the summer. But the sun awakened him early. He stood up and scratched himself, studying his surroundings to find ways in which he might increase his comfort for the nights to come. He would rig up some sort of sunshade, and perhaps re-coil the ropes into the shape of a great doughnut and sleep with his head on one side, his legs thrown over the other, and his rump in the hole. The project preoccupied him so that he forgot why it was he'd spent the night away from home.

But walking up China Lane for breakfast with Miss Anna, he saw once again the changes he'd seen the night before. And there were more of them now: the trees and plants had been affected, too. Many of the lower fronds had turned brown on the coconut trees and the bougainvillaea over the front porch was nearly bare of both leaf and blossom.

Worst of all, when he went back to feed the chickens, he found them under a spell. But of course the poor things, being too stupid to realize the seriousness of their situation, behaved in a perfectly normal way, pecked and scrapped and chattered and preened same as ever, obviously not even knowing the very air they moved through was an invisible prison under the control of Mr. Bolts.

William then turned toward the back door. Approaching with caution, he was relieved to see that the kitchen, protected perhaps by Miss Anna's fine presence in it so much of the time, had not yet been affected. Certain objects of course he knew to be dangerous; for instance, on the drainboard was an angry, scowling teapot he wouldn't have touched for the life of him.

When Miss Anna came down to make breakfast, she seemed not to have been aware of his absence in the night. Nor did she appear to have any sense of what was happening to her house. In fact, she walked right over to the drainboard and touched the tray with the terrible teapot on it, making it perfectly clear to William that his mother shared the same ignorance that prevailed in the hen house.

He studied her carefully for signs of damage and noticed for the first time that she'd lost a lot of her pretty pink fatness and even had some scrawny patches on her. Under her chin he saw a turkey wattle that was new, and as she stirred the pancake batter, her upper arm shook like a half-empty sack with something liquid rolling back and forth in the bottom of it.

And so, while the devil throve upstairs, William's beloved Miss Anna was becoming an old lady, perhaps even dying, and there seemed to be nothing he could do about it, nothing at all.

Until, finally, there came a certain Sunday morning in October.

Miss Anna came downstairs in an unusual state of high spirits. For a thrilling moment, William supposed Mr. Bolts must have died to bring such merriment to her face. But then he discovered it was only a dream she'd had. Still laughing over it, she related it to him:

She goes out to the chicken coop to kill a hen for the pot and finds instead an old rooster there, a dried-up homely thing, useless for frying but just right for soup. She picks him up by the head and neck and walks into the yard with him, swinging him round and round, four, five, six times, until he's good and killed. Then tossing him into the pot, she discovers the old rooster is wearing glasses. Closer scrutiny reveals him to be none other than Mr. Bolts.

William said he thought he'd pass up any soup made with that kind of a bird, and Miss Anna laughed over this remark as if it had contained all the humor under the sun. William tried to laugh along with her, but in the midst of this halfhearted effort a thought took hold of him that brought him to a sudden silence.

Miss Anna, finding herself laughing all alone, began at

once to cry instead. In a matter of seconds her face was a network of tear rivers.

"Oh William," she said, "it was so nice to be laughin' like before." The thought made her cry some more. "'Member how we used to laugh in this kitchen, and laugh and *laugh*? My face'd hurt me so I couldn't stand it. But we'd go right on laughin'." She got to her feet and thrust her chin forward and began cracking eggs into a bowl. "We will again, too!" She shook a fist at the ceiling, her eyes cast in the direction of the sickroom. "Mr. Nuts-'n'-Bolts better watch his p's and q's, 'cause we know what to do with him, make soup out of him!" She was trying hard to invoke the spirit of mirth in the place once more. "Old Buzzard Soup! Isn't that right, William?"

William said, "Yes, ma'am." But he hadn't been listening to a word she said.

When Miss Anna had fed Mr. Bolts and given William his breakfast, she got ready for her one outing of the week, Sunday service at the Grace Evangelical Truth Church. She put on her navy-blue dotted-swiss dress and white pumps, pinned on her white sailor hat with the red ribbon, dabbed her lips with strawberry rouge, stuck a handkerchief in her purse and ten pennies for the collection basket (a dime, when you dropped it in, hardly even clinked, but pennies made a real racket) and stepped out the front door.

William, as usual on Sunday morning since the advent of Mr. Bolts, was stationed in her wicker chair listening for the sound of cowbells from the upstairs room. Lately, instead of sitting on the porch, he had taken to moving the chair into the yard in order to avoid contact with the tainted house.

On this particular morning, for a reason so unclear to

Miss Anna as to be no reason at all, she went over to stand next to him, wondering if she could get away with giving him a kiss on the cheek. Since they were not a kissing family, she was hesitant. Pretending to fuss with the contents of her pocketbook, she stole a long glance at him, assaying her chances; and she noticed something about him that caused her to let out a cry of pain:

He was ordinary.

Her sweet William was nothing but a long, lanky lunk of a workman with his teeth going bad in front, signs of receding hair, lips that were dry and cracked and parted because of some minor difficulty in breathing through his nose, and a faintly mottled complexion with big pores. While none of these aspects of him was new, she had never before seen them so clearly. The William thing in him was absent.

In a flash she saw this double image, the plain man before her, and the William she remembered, a certain quality almost of holiness that had heretofore been apparent in his every feature, in his skin, some soft, unearthly light it gave off, in his hair, the way it grew, in the curve of his back when he was seated, in the easy, loose-jointed way he moved and walked, in his hands which had an extra tenderness in their touch. Even his clothing had been imbued with it and all the objects he habitually used or handled.

Her cry caused William to look up. His eyes, gray-blue and big as ever, were as shiny and empty as a doll's.

"Oh," she said, "I thought I'd lost my, uh . . ." She thrust her right hand and all of her attention deep into her pocketbook. "But here it is!"

She took out her handkerchief and waved it, then rushed down the walk toward the lane, sending out excited little tack-hammer sounds as her heels clicked against the bricks.

By walking very fast and keeping her attention on walking and nothing else, Miss Anna managed to contain her tears until she was settled into her pew. As she wept, she prayed, prayed harder than ever before in her life, prayed for the return of William.

And felt, almost at once, that her prayer would be answered. For, even as she was wiping her nose, a simple plan came into her head from out of nowhere:

She would go home immediately after church and telephone Dr. MacMurtree, tell him to get Mr. Bolts out of her house before nightfall, no matter what. And if the old devil should die the very next morning, so much the better. The loss of the thousand dollars would be her penance, and if the Lord was good, William would . . .

Oh, and the Lord was good, He was He was He was.

She saw it all now. As Mr. Bolts was being hauled up the lane in the ambulance, out of their lives for good and forever, William would be standing on the front porch. He'd take out his jew's harp and begin ever so softly and slowly to play it again, and soon there'd be music more enchanted than any ever heard before. Weather would change, breezes would blow, flowers would bloom, the world would be brought back to its old fine humor. In her enthusiasm she saw a kind of parade taking place, and William, with that William thing restored to him, would be the leader of it. His jew's harp, grown in her mind to the size of a lyre, would make a music that filled not only China Lane but the entire air of the island. For the first time in months, every shutter in town would be thrown open, heads would come peeking out, ears aflap with listening, eyes agog with seeing, and hearts aquiver with the wonder of William returned.

Miss Anna could hardly wait to place the telephone call that would work all this magic. Part of her bargain with God called for her to remain on her knees until the last hymn was sung. But she excused herself from it and left the church.

Back home at a few minutes after eleven, Miss Anna, standing at the door of Mr. Bolts's room, knew the thrill of a gambler who'd hit a lucky streak. Never in her life had she seen such a powerful demonstration of the effectiveness of prayer.

This is how it happened: Coming from the church, she'd hurried up the path toward the porch, wondering idly where William was. Inside, still moving toward the telephone in the parlor, she'd called his name a number of times, but there was no answer. Then, counter to her plan, she found herself walking right past the telephone and up the stairs to the sickroom.

Even as she was opening the door, Miss Anna caught the feel of Mr. Bolts's absence. His body was still there, of course, but it was all tangled in bed sheets, giving to his form the bandaged look of a King Tut.

After her first quick surge of pleasure at the big win, followed quickly by a feeling of awe in the presence of God's power, Miss Anna began at once to feel suspicious of her good fortune.

For one thing she had learned in a lifetime of negotiating deals with God that He seldom behaved in such a direct, openhanded fashion. In fact, she knew Him to be a cagey and unpredictable customer, if not downright sneaky.

In any case, in the present instance, Miss Anna was far from getting down on her knees to thank Him.

Instead she went over to the corpse and untangled its head from the sheet, wondering how she could have failed to notice when Mr. Bolts was alive that his eyes were cast in two separate directions: one aimed at the ceiling, the other at herself. She closed the latter first, and quickly; and when she had closed the second, her own gaze fell at once to Mr. Bolts's throat.

The bruises on it were purple and red and green. And they were brand-new.

A screen door slammed downstairs.

Miss Anna closed the door of the death room and went to the stairway.

William stood on the bottom tread, looking up at her. Their eyes met and held for a long time. Miss Anna's mouth was wide-open and she was hardly breathing at all. After a moment she said, "Oh William," in a barely audible voice, then moved slowly down the stairs, still studying him with intense concentration. She stopped three steps above him so that her eyes were on a level with his. He seemed haunted, and because of this, the question she was about to ask got no farther than the tip of her tongue.

William was a person who could never be counted on to lie.

"Fetch me a glass of water, William," she said.

He went to the kitchen and drew a glass of water. When he returned to the parlor, he found his mother seated awkwardly on the bottom step, skirt hiked up and knees naked, given over to hard, deep thought. She took the glass from him and held it for a long time without drinking from it. William stood a few feet from her, and for a long time they seemed to be frozen at this distance from one another.

Finally, using one hand for leverage, Miss Anna pulled herself to her feet, swallowed the water in one gulp, wiped her mouth on the back of her hand and went to the telephone. She spoke Dr. MacMurtree's number into it.

After a moment, she said, "Dr. Mac . . ." But something was caught in her throat. She cleared it quickly, then blurted out as if it were one word, "Dr. MacMurtree its Anna Bramer he's dead." It was necessary to repeat the information: "Mr. Bolts is dead." There was a pause, and she said, "While I was at church. Now who's going to phone them people in Naples, you?" After a moment, she said, "Well, when you come, don't forget the certificate. The *death* certificate." And finally, sounding rather cross, she said, "Of course finish your coffee! But don't dawdle, for the lord's sake." Then she hung up.

"All right, William," she said, all business, clapping her hands together and not looking at him. "It's gonna be a busy time here, what with doctors and undertakers running in and out. Why don't you just go on downtown and pass the afternoon with your friends, why don't you."

William started at once toward the door, which she held open for him, hurrying as if he'd been caged.

As he passed her, Miss Anna did something that surprised her no less than the sight she'd found upstairs a few minutes earlier:

She spoke his name sharply, "William!"

He stopped walking, and before she knew what was happening, she'd slapped his face. Then she said, "Oh, dear heaven!"

William touched his face, more in surprise than hurt.

Miss Anna said, "I'm sorry, but I'm your mama, William. Can you forgive me?"

He said, "Yes, ma'am, can I go now?"

"Yes, go on," she said, and when he'd reached the lane, she called after him, "See that you're back here by supper!"

When Dr. MacMurtree came up the walk an hour and a half later, Miss Anna met him on the porch, arms akimbo, saying how glad she was he'd taken his good old time getting there. Miss Anna felt she had to act huffy as a way of hiding her shaking.

The doctor laughed at her and said, "I was just giving the old bastard time to cool." Then he went upstairs.

Miss Anna's heart was beating at an abnormal rate and her mouth was dry. She went to the kitchen for a drink of water, then set herself the task of making some limeade, just to keep busy. He seemed to be taking forever up there. Miss Anna had always disliked the slowness of men: at times like this, they infuriated her.

Finally, hearing his footsteps on the stairs, she took the ice tongs and carried the ice to the sink and began chopping at it with the pick. The doctor came into the kitchen and sat at the table. Miss Anna kept her eyes averted.

"I'm makin' limeade," she said.

The doctor took off his glasses and began to rub his eyes.

Miss Anna, waiting for him to say something, put the ice away, poured sugar into the pitcher with the juice, stirred it all carefully, filled it with water, and felt like throwing the whole thing in his face.

Instead she suddenly spoke: "Well, where's that damn death certificate? Didn't you bring it?" And sounded, even to herself, much too impatient.

He waved his hand at her in a way that told her not

to rush him. Then he put his glasses back on and crossed his old schoolboy legs.

"Anna," he said, "you better tell me what happened."

Miss Anna made a face of disgust and showed it to him as she crossed the room for a dish towel. Then she said crossly, "What a fool question! He died, Harold. That's what happened!"

Then she noticed the doctor hadn't bothered to call her Miss Anna, and she'd called him by his first name, without even meaning to. The fact was both comforting and alarming.

"Where was William?" he said.

Miss Anna no longer hid herself. She turned to him at once and met his eyes. Her face was fierce, she seemed suddenly to be a head taller, formidable, perhaps even dangerous. "William was settin' in the yard," she said. Then her eyes changed. Long years of friendship showed in them, but other things as well: a plea, a command, perhaps even some sort of threat. Clearest of all was the determination to stand there looking at him for as long as it might be required of her, forever if necessary.

But after only a few seconds, Dr. MacMurtree took the medical examiner's form from his shirt pocket and spread it out on the table. His eyes had softened, but he was careful to put some harshness into his voice as he asked for her fountain pen.

The afternoon passed quickly. The undertaker's wagon hauled Mr. Bolts away. Miss Anna cleaned out his room, getting rid of all signs of its occupant. Then she had a good soak in the bathtub and, determined never again to wear white, she put on a pretty yellow housedress and a clean, starched apron.

She made a delicious pork stew and put a chocolate cake in the oven. While it was baking, at just about sunset, she heard William out back with the hens. She took out some plates and set them on the table, and by the time William came in at the back door there was a warm, chocolate smell all through the house.

"Them chickens is all right now, I b'lieve," he said.

Often Miss Anna had no notion of what he was talking about, but she answered him just the same. "Oh, that's good," she said.

As she was dishing up the stew, Miss Anna asked, as casually as she could, "Where's y'jew's harp these days?"

"I ain't seen it," he said.

"Well! I declare!" Miss Anna stole a glance at him. His eyes were wide-open, and there were dark circles around them; he seemed to be staring out at her from within a dark cave, wondering what was outside but afraid to move into the light.

"I expect it must of fell through a hole in m'pocket," he said.

Miss Anna clucked her tongue at him.

As they went on with the meal, she became aware that, what with the chewing and the swallowing and the sounds of cutlery hitting plates, eating could certainly be a noisy affair.

She got up and put the radio on.